C000000356

COLD MERCY

DI SARA RAMSEY #10

M A COMLEY

JEAMEL PUBLISHING LIMITED

New York Times and USA Today bestselling author M A Comley
Published by Jeamel Publishing limited
Copyright © 2020 M A Comley
Digital Edition, License Notes

All rights reserved. This book or any portion thereof may not be reproduced, stored in a retrieval system, transmitted in any form or by any means electronic or mechanical, including photocopying, or used in any manner whatsoever without the express written permission of the author, except for the use of brief quotations in a book review or scholarly journal.

This is a work of fiction. Names, characters, places and incidents are a product of the author's imagination or are used fictitiously, and any resemblance to actual persons living or dead, business establishments, events or locales is entirely coincidental.

ACKNOWLEDGMENTS

Thank you as always to my rock, Jean, I'd be lost without
you in my life.

Special thanks as always go to @studioenp for their superb cover
design expertise.

My heartfelt thanks go to my wonderful editor Emmy Ellis, my
proofreaders Joseph, Barbara and Jacqueline for spotting all the
lingering nits.

Thank you also to my amazing ARC group who help to keep me sane
during this process.

To Mary, gone, but never forgotten. I hope you found the peace you
were searching for my dear friend.

ALSO BY M A COMLEY

Blind Justice (Novella)

Cruel Justice (Book #1)

Mortal Justice (Novella)

Impeding Justice (Book #2)

Final Justice (Book #3)

Foul Justice (Book #4)

Guaranteed Justice (Book #5)

Ultimate Justice (Book #6)

Virtual Justice (Book #7)

Hostile Justice (Book #8)

Tortured Justice (Book #9)

Rough Justice (Book #10)

Dubious Justice (Book #11)

Calculated Justice (Book #12)

Twisted Justice (Book #13)

Justice at Christmas (Short Story)

Justice at Christmas 2 (novella)

Justice at Christmas 3 (novella)

Prime Justice (Book #14)

Heroic Justice (Book #15)

Shameful Justice (Book #16)

Immoral Justice (Book #17)

Toxic Justice (Book #18)

Overdue Justice (Book #19)

The Dead Can't Speak (DI Sara Ramsey #3)

Deluded (DI Sara Ramsey #4)

The Murder Pact (DI Sara Ramsey #5)

Twisted Revenge (DI Sara Ramsey #6)

The Lies She Told (DI Sara Ramsey #7)

For The Love Of… (DI Sara Ramsey #8)

Run For Your Life (DI Sara Ramsey #9)

Cold Mercy (DI Sara Ramsey #10) Coming Dec 2020

I Know The Truth (A psychological thriller)

The Caller (co-written with Tara Lyons)

Evil In Disguise – a novel based on True events

Deadly Act (Hero series novella)

Torn Apart (Hero series #1)

End Result (Hero series #2)

In Plain Sight (Hero Series #3)

Double Jeopardy (Hero Series #4)

Criminal Actions (Hero Series #5)

Regrets Mean Nothing (Hero #6)

Sole Intention (Intention series #1)

Grave Intention (Intention series #2)

Devious Intention (Intention #3)

Merry Widow (A Lorne Simpkins short story)

It's A Dog's Life (A Lorne Simpkins short story)

Cozy Mystery Series

Murder at the Wedding

Murder at the Hotel

Murder by the Sea

A Time To Heal (A Sweet Romance)

A Time For Change (A Sweet Romance)

High Spirits

The Temptation series (Romantic Suspense/New Adult Novellas)

Past Temptation

Lost Temptation

Tempting Christa (A billionaire romantic suspense co-authored by Tracie Delaney #1)

Avenging Christa (A billionaire romantic suspense co-authored by Tracie Delaney #2)

PROLOGUE

*A*utumn had arrived early in Hereford, although looking around him today, at the sun bathing his fields with its warm glow, Danny felt good to be alive. This time of the year was a busy time for farmers, moving their livestock from field to field, making good use of the nutrients left which nature had to offer before the winter set in.

"Danny, have you seen my notebook?" Gillian shouted from the kitchen at the end of the hallway.

"Not since last night. You had it in the lounge, have you moved it since then?"

"No. Damn, I can't remember. Can you have a look for me? I'm running late as it is."

"If I have to," he muttered impatiently. He entered the lounge and threw the papers on the sofa aside. Buried beneath was the sought-after notebook. He carried it into the kitchen and dropped it on the pine table, still full of breakfast dishes. "Here it is. Are you going to clear this mess up before you go?"

"I hadn't planned on doing it, no. Can't you wash the dishes this morning? It wouldn't hurt you to help out around here now and again, love."

"What? Do you have any idea how many hours I put in every week?"

Gillian raised a hand and issued a taut smile. "All right. Let's not get bogged down with an argument. I neither have the time nor inclination. I need to be at the hairdresser's at nine-fifteen." She glanced at her watch. "Shit! I should have left ten minutes ago. Thanks for finding my notebook. Sue wanted me to jot down a few recommendations for her, you know, other farms in the area who offered accommodation. A member of her family wants to visit the area soon and would prefer to stay on a farm. She's an animal lover apparently, goes squishy over lambs. Maybe it's something we should consider doing."

"Doing? As in, opening up our home to complete strangers for them to criticise it? Have you cast an eye around here lately, it's hardly the Ritz, is it?"

"And whose fault is that?"

"I do my best, you know I do. I'm not to blame for the price of lamb dropping to an all-time low. Jesus!"

"Exactly. Which is why we need to diversify. Most farmers have had to change the way they work in order to survive. You need to stop being so stubborn and burying your head in the sand, otherwise we'll end up losing this farm, and then where will we be and what will you do for a living? Farming is all you know."

"Exactly. So why start harping on about this diversification malarky?"

Gillian tutted and shook her head. "I give up. You need to sort yourself out. My wage alone isn't going to keep this place running."

"You could go full-time instead of only working a measly eighteen hours a week."

"Hardly. I work more hours than that most weeks, filling in for those who can ruddy well afford to go on holiday."

"Stop complaining, woman. You and the kids do all right."

"Yeah, because of the salary I bring in and *only* because of that."

"Says you. Anyway, I thought you were running late."

"Cutting me off all the time isn't going to solve the problem,

Danny. We need to sit down together and have a serious talk about our finances, and soon."

"We will. Go. I'll even clear up this mess if it'll stop you nagging me."

"I knew I'd grind you down sooner or later. Right, I'm off. Don't get up to no good while I'm out."

"I won't. If I'm not around when you get back, I'll be shifting the flock up to the higher ground later on this morning."

"Take your mobile with you."

"Darn thing. I'll take it as long as you promise not to ring me unless it's a life-or-death situation."

"Same old. I got the message years ago when I bought you the damn thing. It's for emergencies only, make sure it's charged before you set off."

"And stop treating me like a child. Now go, get out of my hair."

"Talking of which, do you want me to make an appointment with Toni to trim yours?"

"Nope. I'm going for the hippy style. At least one of us is conscious of hanging on to what's left in the bank."

Gillian pulled a face at him and leaned forward to kiss him on the cheek. "See you later. Behave yourself while I'm gone. I'll nip to the supermarket while I'm in town, the pantry is looking a bit bare."

"Money, money, spend, spend, that's all you seem to do."

"Bloody charming, I do not! We have to eat, the kids have healthy appetites, and so do you, come to that."

"It's all that fresh air."

"So stop whinging about it."

"I'm not. Go."

Gillian snatched her handbag off the kitchen table and smiled. "Don't forget to do the dishes before you head off."

"Shouldn't that be me telling you that? Whatever, we're going around in circles. Go, enjoy yourself."

"I intend to. See you around lunchtime. I might even pick up one of those special pork pies you like."

"Why not? That'll be nice. A decent lunch other than a ham sarnie will go down a treat. I'll walk you to the car. Talking of which, did the garage say when you can pick yours up?"

"Sometime tomorrow, they were expecting the part to come in today."

"Another way we could cut back, you sell your car and we could both use mine."

Gillian's head shifted from side to side. "No way. I'm not about to give up my independence."

"There you go talking nonsense again. You'll have to give up your independence if we end up taking the route you want to take, to open our home up to visitors." He jabbed his thumb in his chest. "I won't be running around after any guests. That'll be your job. If, and it's a big *if*, we open this place up to a bunch of nosey beaks."

"If we do it, your heart has got to be in it, or it's going to be a waste of time."

He grunted and shooed her out of the door onto the gravelled drive. "A conversation for another time."

"See you later." Gillian opened the door to the old Jaguar his father had handed down to him a few years ago and threw her handbag onto the passenger seat. She waved and closed the door.

He waved and turned his back on her and headed towards the front door.

The blast almost deafened him. The force of it planted him face-down into the gravel. Scrambling to recover, he peered over his shoulder to see his beloved car, with his wife inside, in flames.

"Gillian, Gillian… No! This can't be happening." He clambered to his feet, one arm shielding his face from the heat. He tried to get close to the vehicle, but the temperature was too fierce, and he retreated. "Shit! What do I do?" He ran inside, his head suddenly clearing, and rang nine-nine-nine.

"Hello, which emergency service do you require?"

"I don't know…it's my wife…oh God, please, you have to help me."

"Okay, sir, calm down. Where are you calling from? Can you tell me what's happened?"

"Northcott Farm, out on the Leominster Road. She was on her way out when BOOM! It... God, the car, it's in flames. I can't get near it. Please, someone has to come and help me rescue her. She's inside the car. Please, please, help me!" A sob caught in his throat.

"Okay, I've contacted the fire brigade, and an ambulance is on the way, too."

"Oh, thank you. I need to hang up and see if I can help her now."

"No, sir. Stay on the line and keep away from the fire. Do not, I repeat, do not, go near the vehicle."

"But I have to try to save her."

"As much as I admire you wanting to do that, I can't allow you to put yourself at risk like that. Do you have children?"

"Yes, two. What's that got to do with anything?"

"They're going to need you now more than ever, sir. Do not put yourself in danger, please, think of them."

"Oh God, you're right. Gillian, oh, Gillian, what am I going to do without you?"

"Don't give up hope."

"You haven't seen it. The car is engulfed in flames. Wait, I have a fire extinguisher in the barn." He slammed the phone down and ran through the house like a speeding bullet.

The barn was forty feet away from the fire. He grabbed the extinguisher, carried it across the courtyard and aimed it at the vehicle. It didn't take long for him to retreat. The intense heat was singeing his face and hands.

In the distance, the sound of sirens drifted on the air. It wasn't long before the cherry-red fire engine pulled into the drive. Two firemen grasped his arms and tugged him back, away from the lashing flames.

"What's your name?" one of them asked.

"It's Danny. You don't understand. My wife is in that!" He pointed at the car, melting before their eyes.

"Let's get you inside. Our men will deal with this. Come on."

He shrugged their hands off and took two paces forward before the two burly firemen gripped his arms again and escorted him into the house. Danny peered over his shoulder, feeling numb, unable to speak as the shock set in.

They placed him in a chair at the kitchen table while one of them filled the kettle and switched it on. "You need a nice cup of sweet tea."

He shook his head. "No. I don't want it. All I want is my wife. Go out there and save her."

The two firemen glanced at each other.

The older one slapped a gloved hand on his shoulder. "I'm sorry, mate. There's no way your wife, or anyone else for that matter, could have survived that blaze."

Danny buried his head in his hands and sobbed openly for the first time in his life. Then he muttered her name over and over. "Gillian, Gillian, Gillian…"

1

---

*S*ara stretched and ran her hand down her husband's back. "Morning, are you awake?"

"I wasn't, but guess what? I am now." He turned over to smile at her.

She leaned in for a kiss. "I think I've had the best night's sleep ever in my thirty-four years on this earth."

"Any reason why?" He placed his head next to hers on the pillow.

"Because I'm so happy, and that's down to you, Mark Fisher. Wonderful man that you are."

"Get away with you, it takes a combined effort to make a relationship work, and we'll always be equal partners."

"Yep. Oh well, that's our honeymoon over. It was fantastic while it lasted, but it's back to the grind today."

"I was thinking about that…why don't we make it a yearly thing, going up to Scotland for our anniversary?"

"How romantic of you. If it's doable every year, then yes, I think we should make plans to do it. For now, though, I need to get a wriggle on and see what crimes await me in Hereford."

"Same for me with regard to my schedule. I hope I don't come across too many hissing cats and snappy dogs today, what with it being my first day back."

"You could always take Misty with you to sort them out. Mind you, I think she's still sulking with us after leaving her to go away."

"No, that's your imagination. She's fine. She enjoyed staying with Ted and Mavis, she's probably more annoyed at leaving their comfy home than us deserting her to go on honeymoon."

Sara frowned. "I hadn't thought of it like that. Maybe you're right. Either way, she's been a little mardy with us since we got back on Saturday."

"Give her time to come around."

She kissed him again. "You're such an expert on animal psyche. I bow to your greatness and knowledge."

He laughed. "Now I know you're winding me up."

She flung the quilt back and slipped out of bed. "My shower awaits. I can't remember if I put the boiler on last night or not."

"I did it."

"Thanks."

Thirty minutes later, after eating her scrambled egg on toast and bacon which Mark had prepared for her while she got dressed, she left the house.

"Ring me during the day if you get the chance," he called after her.

"I'll try. Will you be home around six?"

"Hopefully, depends if any emergencies show up. Have a good day."

"You, too." She blew him a kiss and mouthed 'I love you' rather than let the whole close hear the endearment.

It felt strange slipping back into her routine again as a married woman. Here she was, deeply in love and contented for the second time in her life. She pushed away the feeling of dread that always crept in when she thought about it. And prayed nothing would happen to Mark the way tragedy had struck with Philip. She'd make that her life's ambition if necessary, to ensure he remained safe. She couldn't go through that trauma again, ever. There was only so much tragedy a person could handle in their lives, right?

Which reminded her, she would need to check in on her parents later, to see how they were doing after holding her brother's funeral. She was still riddled with guilt for neglecting him once he'd taken the wrong path in life which had ultimately ended in his death. Her happy mood gave way to a sadness that had crept into her honeymoon every now and again. She supposed that was natural, considering her brother had only died a few weeks before. Her mother especially had been devastated by his death. She seemed intent on punishing herself for not caring more about Timothy recently. On the whole, her family had a lot of healing to go through before a sense of normality returned to their lives anytime soon.

As she drew into the car park, she spotted Carla entering the main doors. She parked in her allotted space and followed her partner into the building.

"Morning, Jeff. How have things been in my absence?"

He held his hand out and tilted it from side to side. "Fair to middling, I'd say, ma'am. No need to ask you if you had a wonderful time, it's written all over your face how happy you are."

"I am. I'm just waiting for a case to come along to change all of that." She laughed and punched in her code to gain access to the inner sanctum.

She walked into the incident room to find Carla at the vending machine. "Mine's a coffee, white with one sugar, just in case you've forgotten how I take it."

Carla tutted. "As if I'm likely to forget that within a week. You seem chirpy this morning. I take it you've had a fabulous honeymoon."

"The best time ever. Thanks. How have things been around here?"

"Quiet mostly. It's as if all the criminals went on holiday the same time as you. We had a few minor incidents to deal with, a couple of GBHs and petty burglaries where the proprietors of a nightclub and a post office got attacked, but nothing more than that. Thank goodness. As a team we've been able to get on top of all the paperwork from the previous months' cases. Umm…I tried my best to deal with the post, but it kind of overwhelmed me."

Sara tentatively poked her head around the door and saw a week's worth of brown envelopes waiting for her. "Shit! Okay, you'd better buy me two cups to help me wade through that lot."

"Sorry, I did my best, I promise you."

"No need to apologise. I'll get my head down and start on it ASAP. Hopefully it won't take me long to plough through it. Dare I ask how things are on the home front?"

Carla hitched up a shoulder, and her focus remained on the vending machine as she slotted another coin in. "I moved out. Things got a little heated with Gary, and I made the call that it would be better if we parted. I don't want to be miserable all the time, Sara."

"And you shouldn't be. Someone will come along who will see you for what you are, a kind, caring soul. Don't accept anything but the finest. I know all men start off on their best behaviour; if necessary, you're going to have to fall back on your detective skills and dig deeper from the outset. Believe me, I know how difficult it is doing that, but it's going to be a necessity for you going forward, love."

"Yeah, I suppose you're right. Maybe I should avoid men whose mothers are still alive in the future."

Sara laughed. "If only that were possible. You need to make arrangements to meet the parents on the first date before you get in too deep with someone else."

"Crikey, no pressure there then. Here you go." Carla handed her a steaming cup of coffee.

"Thanks. I'll shout when I want it topping up. Until then, I'll be in my den, sifting through the endless post."

"Sorry. I feel so guilty. I was totally out of my depth."

"Stop apologising. Give me a shout—in other words, come and rescue me—if anything major crops up."

"Will do. I could always come and give you a hand, if you want."

"Go on then, if you're up to date on things around here."

"We are. Sort of. The rest of the team can deal with what's left."

"Bring your drink then."

Sara entered the office, placed her cup on the desk and stopped to admire the view from her window. The low clouds were covering the Brecon Beacons today which disappointed her.

"You love that view, don't you?"

"I do. I feel like I belong here as long as I can see the view. Saying that, the views up in Scotland are magnificent compared to this."

"Don't tell me you're thinking of relocating again?"

"Gosh, no fear of me doing that, not yet anyway. Maybe I'll retire up there, who knows?"

They settled into their chairs on either side of the desk, and Sara sorted through the pile, placing them in different stacks in order of priority. She'd almost finished the task when the phone on her desk rang. Carla answered it.

"DS Jameson, can I help…? Yes, Jeff, she's here. I'll put you on speaker. Go ahead."

"Sorry to trouble you both. I've just heard about an interesting case that I think will be right up your street."

Sara rolled her eyes and made a face as she glanced down at the mess in front of her. "Go on, I guess this post is doomed to remain languishing on my desk, untouched. What are we talking about, Jeff?"

"We've had a call about a car going up in flames out at a farm. The farmer's wife was in the vehicle at the time."

"Accident or intentional?" Sara asked, her interest piquing to a higher level.

"They're not sure at the moment. Do you want it or shall I pass it on to someone else?"

"We'll take it. Carla and I will be down in a tick, you can give us the details then."

"I'll get all the information you need ready for you."

Carla hung up. "I'll see if the rest of the team are here."

"I'll be with you soon. I'll just gather this lot up first."

. . .

*I*t took them over thirty minutes to reach the farm.

"Shit! Just what I need," Carla grumbled as the fire engine came into view.

"Damn. I never thought. Maybe it'll be a different team in attendance. Is Gary even back at work full-time yet after his accident?"

"Yep, he started back last week. He flung the words at me along with my final suitcase."

"Fuck, sorry you had to go through that, love. Shoulders back, ignore him if you can—if he's here, that is."

"He's here." Carla raised her hand and pointed ahead of them, her finger hidden by the dashboard.

"Don't let him get to you. Stick beside me. We'll tackle it together, okay?"

"Thanks, Sara. I'm fine. I won't let him distract me. Looks like they're packing up to go anyway."

"Good. Okay, I've spotted Lorraine's vehicle over there. I'll get as close as possible to it."

She pulled up alongside the pathologist's van. Lorraine greeted them with a wave and a smile and motioned for them to join her.

Sara and Carla togged up in paper suits and headed her way.

"Shit! Gary's seen us," Carla whispered.

"Ignore him. We have every right to be here, the same as he has. His colleagues are doing their best to distract him."

"They're failing. He's coming this way."

Sara instantly swapped sides with her partner and held out a hand to prevent the fireman coming any closer. "All right, Gary, there's no need for you to cause any aggro. We're here to attend the scene, just like you are."

His eyes narrowed, and he bared his teeth at the pair of them. "She's got no right to be here."

Sara pushed against his solid chest. "You know that's not true. Back off or I'll be forced to arrest you."

"For what?" he spat at her.

"Disrupting the peace, aggressive behaviour…I could go on."

"What's going on here?" Gary's boss came storming towards them. "Gary, back away. Leave the ladies to get on with their work."

"I was just..." Gary began. One stern look from his boss and he relented. Turning on his heel, he marched back to be with his colleagues.

"Sorry about that. The split...well, he's taken it badly," his boss apologised awkwardly.

Carla bowed her head. "It was for the best. He's volatile, I didn't feel safe being with him."

Gary's boss rubbed his hand up and down her arm. "I'm sorry you felt that way. It's tough being him right now, the months of rehabilitation he's had to contend with."

"I was there for him every step of the way and yet I received no gratitude for putting my life on hold to care for him. I'm sorry, I couldn't take it any more. I could only see the situation getting worse, not better," Carla replied grimly.

"She has a right to end something if she feels threatened. Maybe you should persuade Gary to see a counsellor. He's clearly unstable," Sara pointed out.

"We'll care for our own, we don't need outsiders telling us where we're going wrong. Thanks, ladies. Enjoy the rest of your day." He grunted and stormed off.

"Shit, I'm sorry you had to go through that, Carla. Are you all right?"

"I'll be fine, once they've packed up and gone."

"Disregard them. Let's see what Lorraine has for us."

The roar of the fire engine pulling away made Carla look behind her.

"Ignore it, hon. You're not doing yourself any favours."

"I know. Bloody hell, I swear, I'm never going to get involved with another man again. Why do I always pick the cruddy ones?"

"There's someone right for you out there. Don't cut yourself off just yet, you're too young for that."

"Are you two joining me or what?" Lorraine bellowed from close to the burnt-out vehicle.

Sara waved and smiled. "Be there in a sec." Turning back to Carla, she asked, "Are you okay to continue? Or would you rather wait in the car?"

"I'm fine. Don't worry about me."

"That's a little hard to do when you're standing right beside me with a face like thunder. Chin up, love."

"I'll be fine. I promise." Carla walked ahead of Sara and reached Lorraine first.

"Nice of you to join us. Can't you carry on your love affair away from the crime scene, Carla?" Lorraine was quick with her inaccurate judgement of what had just taken place.

"Leave it, Lorraine. Don't go there," Sara admonished.

Lorraine's eyes widened. "Have I said something wrong? I was only teasing."

Carla sighed and puffed out her cheeks. "You might as well know, Gary and I split up last week. You just witnessed him wiping the floor with me."

"Ouch! Sorry, chuck. Me and my big mouth." Lorraine held her leg out in front of her. "Kick me if it'll make you feel any better."

The three of them laughed.

"It wouldn't help, but thanks for the offer."

"Right. Let's get down to business. What have we got, Lorraine?" Sara bent to peer into the vehicle and winced as bile surfaced and scorched her throat. "Shit! Did she suffer? Or is that a daft question?"

"That's the question. Logically, I'd predict she didn't. The husband said the car went up the second she started the engine. My take is she wouldn't have felt anything, but that would be a wild guess. Her seat belt was attached; she might've still been alive and panicked as the flames licked at her skin."

"All right, Lorraine, there's no need to go into the gruesome details so soon after breakfast."

Lorraine smiled broadly. "Sorry, bacon sarnie with ketchup, was it?"

Sara rolled her eyes and huffed out a breath. "That's where you're wrong. Scrambled egg on toast with bacon and ketchup."

"Anyway, it's going to take us a while to sift through this lot, so don't expect any results overnight—just warning you in case you have an overwhelming urge to start hounding me for answers."

"When have I ever done that?"

Lorraine shrugged. "There's always a first time. I need to go through the vehicle's service record and other details before we can rule anything out."

"Do cars have a tendency to blow up at the drop of a hat?" Carla asked, scrutinising the car herself and backing up slightly after witnessing the effects of the explosion first-hand.

"Not come across it before. This is an older model, so anything's possible. The husband is inside if you want to have a word with him. There's nothing more I can tell you right now."

"Okay, we'll catch you later. Dare I ask how the hubby is?" Sara asked.

Lorraine gave her the look that told her it was one of the dumbest questions she'd asked in a while. "Go see for yourself."

"Right, will do."

Sara and Carla entered the front door of the house.

Sara called out, "Is anyone here? Mr Jenkinson?"

"In here," a female voice responded from the end of the long narrow hallway.

They made their way through the farmhouse that, Sara imagined, had seen better days. They passed a lounge on the right and a dining room on the left before they walked into a large spacious kitchen that dated back to the nineteen sixties, judging by the design of the cupboards, which all appeared to be freestanding.

Mr Jenkinson was sitting at the kitchen table, his head in his hands and his shoulders shaking as he wept. A female uniformed officer was standing right behind him. There was a cup of black coffee on the table, close to the man who had just lost his wife. Lorraine was right, he appeared distraught. But then, who wouldn't be given the circumstances?

"Hello, Mr Jenkinson, I'm DI Sara Ramsey, and this is my partner,

DS Carla Jameson. Condolences on the loss of your wife, sir. I hate to ask, but are you up to answering a few questions for us?"

"I suppose so. Take a seat." He pulled a brown cotton handkerchief from his pocket and proceeded to blow his nose. "All this has come as a shock to me."

"I can imagine. Can you run through what happened this morning?"

"It was like any other morning in this household, often chaotic with two young kids to get ready for school. My wife had an appointment at the hairdresser's. I was the one who walked the kids to the regular pick-up point up the road. When I came back, Gillian was still faffing about. I helped her search for her notebook and then I saw her off. She used my car...oh God, it could have been me. Why wasn't it me instead of my beautiful wife? I'll never be able to forgive myself for allowing her to get in that car."

"While it's understandable you blaming yourself, sir, it's not going to help you in the long run, is it?"

"I don't know, isn't it? I've never been in this situation before, have you? Sorry, I didn't mean to snap at you."

"It's okay to vent your anger, it's natural. Just bear in mind that we're here to help you."

"I'll try. What else do you want to know?" He wiped the handkerchief across his eyes.

"When you say it was your car, are you telling me you shared it?"

"No, it's my car, or it was. My father left it to me when he passed away five years ago. It's a workhorse. It's never let me down in the past, and yes, I service it properly."

"May I ask why your wife was driving it today?"

"Because her Fiesta is in for repairs, something wrong with the brakes. I told her to use mine instead as I would be busy here today, moving the flock around. Shit! I should be out there doing that now."

"I'm sure the flock can wait a few more hours or days, sir, that appears to be the least of your worries."

"You reckon? If I don't get them shifted soon and the weather turns nasty, that'll be me in trouble for the next few months. Have you seen the weather lately? It's so unpredictable. But a farmer's working life is dependent on how it fares day in, day out."

"I wasn't aware of that. You learn something new every day in this job."

He stared at Sara. "There you go then, your snippet of knowledge for the day. Is it going to bring my wife back? I doubt it. Fuck! Excuse my language, but what the hell am I going to tell the little ones?"

"That's going to be tough. How old are they?"

"Tammy is five, and Ben is six. Tammy is a younger model of my wife. God, every time I mention her, I want to well up again. Is that natural?"

"Of course it is. Do you have any other family living close by?"

Carla took out her notebook, ready to jot down any relevant information if required.

"No, yes, what am I saying? My head's all muddled. My mother, but she's in a nursing home with dementia."

"I'm sorry to hear that."

"Old age creeps up on all of us in the end. She went downhill after Dad died and has continued to deteriorate ever since. She no longer knows who I am. I mourned her loss a few months back, if you must know. I rarely go to see her now because it's too heartbreaking to contend with."

"That's terrible to hear. No other distant relatives nearby?"

"No one. We're not from around here originally, we moved up from Cornwall around ten years ago. Mum and Dad followed us up here, but then Dad became ill and sadly died about five years ago... have I told you that already? I'm sorry for repeating myself if I have, my mind is so messed up. Shit! What about the kids, how am I going to care for them, now that Gillian's gone?"

"What about friends? Did either you or your wife have friends who could possibly help out?"

"Maybe Vanessa will help. Yes, I'll give her a call later. See if she can lend a hand with the kids while I move the sheep."

Sara let the reference to the sheep pass this time round. "Would you like me to give Vanessa a call?"

"God, would you? She's going to be distraught when she hears Gillian has gone. No, maybe I should do it. No, I can't, I wouldn't be able to do it without breaking down. Oh heck, what a mess. Why? Why her? Why now, when I need her the most? Why? Why? Why?" His hands covered his head, and the tears he shed fell onto the table beneath him. He wiped them away then looked up at Sara. "I'm sorry, I feel such a fool. This is so overwhelming, I can't get my head around why this happened. I feel so guilty."

Sara's ears pricked up. "Guilty? Why?"

"Because it was my car, and I should have been driving it when it exploded, that's why."

"Has the car been any bother lately, sir?"

"No. It's been as good as gold. Never once let me down, except... no, that was my fault."

"What was?"

"I ran out of petrol a few months back. We got stranded in one of the back lanes. The wife kicked off, and the kids started screaming. My breakdown cover had lapsed the week before, that's why Gillian was furious with me."

"A combination of things going wrong can be damaging to a relationship, can't it?"

He frowned and glared at her. "What are you saying? It was one bloody incident. Once we'd been rescued and were back here, the equilibrium returned soon enough."

"I wasn't inferring anything. I'm glad you got it sorted in the end. Did a friend come to your rescue?"

"A passerby, a neighbour in the next village actually. He dropped me at a petrol station and ferried me back to my family."

"That was nice of him."

"We farmers need to stick together. We're misunderstood most of the time."

"You are? By whom?"

"Everyone, especially your lot. The number of times I've rung you when one of my ewes has gone missing only to be told you'll look into it but never do. Each ewe is valuable to us. We've had that many break-ins at the farms in the area, too, and your lot just don't want to know. Stamp the small crimes out first, it'll deter the culprits from escalating, but no, the police refuse to get involved. Leaving us high and dry and fending for ourselves. We've got a right to be protected just like those living in the towns, haven't we?"

"Of course you have. I'm sorry you feel as though we've let you down, sir."

"On more than one occasion." He stopped talking and stared at Sara.

"Sir, is something wrong?"

He ran a gnarled hand with mud ingrained in his fingernails over his face. "I should have realised…shit! Why didn't I put two and two together?"

"Sir? Has something happened that we should be aware of?"

"You were aware of it. Your lot chose to ignore it, and now this has fucking happened. Why should I trust you? It's not like you've gone out of your way to help me in the past. And now she's gone. This is down to you, no one else. If you hadn't ignored my pleas for help, none of this would have happened."

"I don't understand. Maybe if you told us what you're talking about."

"The notes I received. I gave them to the copper at the station. He promised me he'd look into it and never got back to me."

"What notes, sir?"

"The threatening notes. The ones sent to me through the post. Gillian forced me to take them to the station about six months ago. I knew I was wasting my time but I did as she suggested and never heard another word from you since."

"DS Jameson, make a note, we'll check on that when we return to the station."

"Will do, boss." Carla scribbled down Sara's request, and Jenkinson watched on.

"What did these notes say?" Sara asked.

"They threatened me. Told me I was next."

"Next?"

"Yes, the person killed one of my pregnant ewes, nailed her to a tree and left the unborn foetus hanging out of the ewe's womb."

"That's disgusting. How have these threats manifested themselves?"

"Just the notes and slaughtering my sheep so far, well, and this…I suppose we should take Gillian's death into consideration as well now."

"It does sound like it was an intentional act from what you've told us already. My next question is, who? Who do you believe is behind all of this?"

He stared at his hands, clenched and unclenched them a few times. "I don't know. Do you think if I knew that I wouldn't have strung the bastard up by now? They've set out to do what they intended and ruined my sodding life and my livelihood to boot, I shouldn't wonder. I'm not going to be able to concentrate on the farm full-time now, not with looking after my kids as well. Shit! Why me? Why us? Gillian, she didn't deserve to go out like this, why her?"

"I'm not sure anyone deserves to go out that way. You have my assurance that we'll get to the bottom of this. There's sure to be some form of evidence for us to work from out there."

He glanced out of the window and shook his head. "I doubt it, everything went up in flames…including my wife." His voice fell to a whisper at the end, and he broke down again.

"I'm so sorry. This is tough to handle, I know it is. Try to remain positive for your kids' sake. We're on the case now. I can't apologise enough for the way my colleagues have treated you. I want to assure you that we'll deal with your case with the utmost professionalism. We'll catch whoever is guilty of disrupting your life with these threats and possibly killing your wife. I'm afraid we won't be able to call it 'murder' yet, not until the pathologist has conducted a post-mortem and typed up her report with her findings."

He placed a clenched hand over his heart. "I feel it here. I know she was killed. I want this bastard caught and punished swiftly before he does any further damage to my livestock, my property, or my family, come to that."

"As do we. Sir, the more you can tell us the better at this stage. We need to get the investigation underway and quickly. I know I'm asking a lot of you, given that you're grieving the loss of your wife, but anything you can tell us would be better than nothing at all."

"What else can I tell you? I don't know anything else."

"You say these threats or notes began appearing around six months ago, is that correct?"

"Give or take, yes, that's right."

"Can you recall falling out with anyone around that time? Someone who you think would be likely to take revenge on your actions towards them?"

"A few people, yes. I'm not the type to suffer fools gladly. If people do the dirty on me...well, you know, I want nothing further to do with them."

"Would you care to elucidate?"

"Not really. It should be self-explanatory."

"Okay, we'll come back to that. These people, can you give us their names?"

Sighing, he glanced out of the window again, to what remained of his car, and his wife. "My neighbours on both sides. Andy Brady and Frank Dobbs."

"Is there a reason you fell out with both of them at the same time?"

"Not really. They're thick as thieves, those two. What one does, the other is sure to do, too. If Andy was to run around naked in his acreage for half a day, Frank would have no hesitation in doing the same." He smiled at his own joke. His expression quickly changed to a more thunderous one when he looked Sara's way again. "They take the piss. Call me names."

"What sort of names?"

"Everything under the sun most days."

"Why?"

He shrugged, and his mouth turned down at the sides. "Who knows?"

"There must be a reason why their behaviour changed towards you in the past six months, sir. Please try and think."

"I can't. I've been wracking my brains for bloody months. They're just country bumpkins who think they know better than a damn townie."

"Ah, I see. They object to you taking up a farming role, is that it?"

"I think so. Life is difficult enough for farmers these days as it is, without falling out with your neighbours. I told them we should be pulling together, trying to make a success, helping each other out in times of need, and they gave me the two fingers, told me to sod off back to the city where I belonged."

"Sorry to hear that. But why now? Or have they always resented you and your family being here?"

"No. Oh, I can't remember when things took a turn for the worst. They started off amicable enough. Helped out when I asked their opinion on things. I always helped in return where I could, then…they didn't want to know."

"Because you'd become established, could that be the reason, sir? Able to exist without their help, is that it?"

"I haven't got the foggiest. You'll have to direct that question to them, not me. I might be talented in certain areas, but mind-reading isn't a forte of mine." He chuckled and then grew sombre again, almost instantly.

"We'll be sure to call on them either today or tomorrow, see what they both have to say."

"Tomorrow! Are you crazy?" he shouted. "You should be over there now. See, you're going to be just like your colleagues, aren't you? Not willing to accept my word on things. What if they do a runner? Fuck off before you've had a chance to tackle them about all of this, what then?"

"You're right. I'll correct my statement and promise you that we'll pay each of them a visit straight after we leave here."

"Good. People as vile as that shouldn't be able to get away with things of this nature."

"I wholeheartedly agree. We'll question them to see what they have to say."

"Shouldn't you do that now, while the iron is hot, so to speak?"

"After we've got what we need from you, sir." Sara smiled tautly. "Perhaps you can give us a few more details about the disputes you've been having with them first."

"They were about something and nothing, really."

"Can you give me an example?"

"Land disputes mainly. Them pinching a few feet of my land along each of the boundaries, as though it's a conspiracy against me and my family. That may not sound much to you, but land is turning into a valuable commodity nowadays. Worth far more than it used to be, that's for sure."

"I was unaware of that. And they've both been guilty of stealing some land from you?"

He nodded once.

"Have you informed the council about this?"

"What's the point? They're just like your lot. Present them with the evidence, and they shove it in a desk drawer somewhere, never to see the light of day again. Sickening. We're talking about someone's damn livelihood at the end of the day, and no one in authority gives a flying fuck about it."

Sara puffed out her cheeks. "I can't keep apologising for what's gone on in the past, all I can do is assure you that things will change going forward."

"So you say. In the meantime, my wife has just died, and someone is guilty of ripping this family apart. I hope for your sake they don't get away with it, although, judging by what's gone on in the past, they bloody will."

Sara couldn't keep going over the same ground with him. It was obvious he was seething about the way he'd been treated, and rightly so, in her opinion.

"Is there anyone else you'd like to put on the list, Mr Jenkinson?"

His head bowed, and he wrung his hands. "I don't think so, my head is a bit fuzzy now. I've had enough of going around and around in circles. I need to move my flock and prepare myself for what lies ahead, informing my kids their mother is no longer with us. Any suggestions how I break that kind of news to a five- and six-year-old?" His hand slicked through his longish blond hair.

"I'm sorry, I have no experience in that department. Maybe you can delay things until everything is clearer in your own mind first."

"And maybe I'll just tell them their mother is visiting a relative for now. That might solve the problem."

"Whatever suits you best, sir. Okay, I think we have enough here to be going on with. I'll leave you my card. Please, ring me if you think of anything else you feel might be important. I'll be in touch during the case to let you know our progress." She slid a card across the table towards him.

He picked it up and looked at it, then propped it against the salt pot in the middle of the table. "Thanks."

The three of them rose from their chairs.

Sara smiled at the uniformed officer. "A quick word if I may?" She went into the hallway with the officer while Carla remained in the kitchen with Jenkinson. "Keep a close eye on him. Make sure he doesn't harm himself."

"Oh God, I hadn't thought of that, ma'am. Of course I will, while he's around here. What should I do if he's out in the fields tending his sheep?"

"That's another matter. Try and stay as close to him as you can."

"Okay, I'll do that. Horrendous ordeal. I feel sorry for him and what's ahead of them as a family."

"I agree. It's going to be far from easy for him to contend with. Maybe if his children were older things might be different. Here's my card. If anything comes up that you think I should hear about, ring me, day or night, got that?"

"Yes, ma'am. How long do you think I'll be expected to stay here?"

"A few days minimum. Have a word with the duty sergeant. I want someone here with him around the clock. I'm not saying I expect you to be on duty twenty-four-seven, but someone else needs to take over from you. At least for a few days."

"I'll contact the boss as soon as he goes off to tend to his flock in that case. I don't mind being here, glad to help out in the circumstances. Maybe I can ease it for him when the kids finally come home from school."

"Maybe. My advice would be to stand back until he asks for help in that department. How are your culinary skills?"

"Passable. Is that expected of me? To cook their meals for them?"

"No, not in the slightest. All I'm thinking is if you want to assist them, helping to put food on the table would ease the burden on his shoulders right now. I'll leave that with you."

"I'll consider it, ma'am. I'm not really what you'd call a good cook. No doubt I can manage to rustle up beans on toast for the kids, if that's what he wants."

"Good. Any problems, ring me, okay?" she felt the need to repeat.

"I'll do that."

She dismissed the PC with a smile, and the young officer returned to the kitchen. Carla appeared in the hallway a few seconds later. They left the house.

"Hi, Lorraine, I know this is going to be a difficult one to call, but after speaking with the husband, he's under the impression that we're dealing with a malicious act," Sara said.

"Did he give you a name?"

"Two men he's fallen out with over the past few months. We're on our way to see them now."

"Good luck with that." Lorraine peered at the sky. "Thank God the weather is with us today, it's been changeable lately. We'll do the necessary here and then shoot off. Don't expect to hear from me anytime soon with the results."

"I won't. I know what's in store for you. Just get them to me as soon as you can."

"That goes without saying. Break a leg, ladies."

"Thanks. I think we're going to need all the help we can muster on this one. Speak soon."

At the car, Sara and Carla stripped off their protective suits and placed them in the awaiting black sack.

Sara started up the engine and exited the drive before she spoke. "I have a feeling this one is going to be super difficult to solve."

"You took the words out of my mouth. Would neighbours truly resort to such underhand tactics?"

"I'm not sure. I suppose anything is possible in the right circumstances. I got the impression that Danny Jenkinson is a tough person to deal with."

"You got that from one grief-stricken conversation with the man?"

"Are you telling me I'm wrong to say that?"

"No, I'm just amazed at you coming right out and mentioning it, that's all."

"It is what it is. I think we should tread carefully with the two neighbours to begin with. No point getting their backs up from the outset. I'd rather go in there softly-softly, see what their take is on what has gone on with their friendship, than go in there accusing them of all sorts right out of the starting gate."

"I agree. I feel sorry for the kids. How the hell is he going to be able to run the farm single-handedly and bring up two young kids with no wife to support him?"

"At least he's alive to do it. Ouch, that sounded heartless even to my ears. Sorry, I shouldn't have said that. It's the truth, though. If his wife hadn't got in that car today, well, he wouldn't be around to care for the kids, and it would be the wife we'd be showing sympathy to, wouldn't it?"

"You're right, as usual. It doesn't alter the fact that there are two little humans who will be devastated by the loss of a parent when the school kicks out later."

"*If* he sits them down to talk to them. I've got a feeling he'll dodge that bullet, for today at least. He'll have to tell them soon. I don't envy him that task at all."

"Me neither. We're here. This is Wyle Farm." Carla pointed at the sign nailed to the stone wall outside the courtyard.

Sara nodded and pulled up next to a Land Rover caked in dried mud. Soon after, a man dressed in a white checked shirt, jeans and a padded body warmer emerged from the farmhouse. He marched towards them, his eyes narrowed in suspicion, and stood next to the car.

"Who are you?"

Sara and Carla exited the vehicle and produced their IDs.

"DI Sara Ramsey and DS Carla Jameson, and you are?"

"Andy Brady. And what brings the police to my door then?" he said, his tone brusque.

"We'd like to ask you a few questions about your neighbours, if you have the time, sir."

He glanced at his watch. "I have a delivery arriving in half an hour. I can spare you twenty minutes, if that'll do."

"That should be enough. Can we go inside?" Sara pressed her key fob, locking the car.

He pointed back to the farmhouse and gave a brief nod. "If you want. Come this way."

Sara and Carla entered the house after Brady. He led them into the kitchen which was warmed by a huge red range cooker.

"Want a coffee, do you? Or a tea?"

"Two coffees, white with one sugar, thanks very much," Sara replied.

"Take a seat. How do you prefer it?"

"As it comes, medium for me."

"And for me," Carla added.

Brady filled the kettle and placed it on top of the range to boil. "It'll take a good five minutes to heat up, sorry for the delay." He sat in a spare chair and folded his arms. "What's this all about then?"

"Are you aware of something that happened earlier today?"

"I was out there and heard a loud bang, if that's what you're talking about. What was it? Nothing new coming from Jenkinson's farm."

"Meaning what, Mr Brady?"

"Call me Andy, you don't need to stand on ceremony in my house, lass."

Sara detected a slight Scottish accent. "Have you lived around here long?"

He laughed. "I see your detective skills are top notch. I moved down from the Highlands around twenty years ago. The missus said she'd leave me if we didn't up sticks and move to a warmer climate. I didn't mind either way. I suppose it made financial sense to have the cattle out in the fields longer than having to fork out on extra food for them to see them through the winter."

"I see. And you both like it around here?"

Carla flipped open to a new page in her notebook. "'Ere, what are you taking down my answers for, lass? Have I done something wrong?"

"It's just procedure, Andy." Sara smiled. "Can I ask what you heard?"

"A loud bang, possibly an explosion. Like a petrol cannister exploding, that sort of thing. I suppose I should be used to it with him. He's a bit of an idiot, if you ask me. Has only been farming, if you can call it that, for the past ten years or so. Still a complete novice in my book. He's one of these know-it-all types. I've tried to offer him the power of my wisdom over the years, but he's more stubborn than a dozen mules put together, that one."

"Is it true to say you don't get along then? With him or with the family?"

"Just him. His wife, Gillian, she's a lovely lady. Nips over here regularly, she does." He wagged his finger and laughed. "Get your mind out of the gutter. She's a good friend of my wife's, she is."

"Ah, I see. Is your wife around?"

"No, she's away for a few days visiting her mother. She had a fall at the weekend and ended up in hospital. They're doing a hip replacement this week. I told Olivia to stay there. I can cope on my own. Anyway, Gillian often brings over a cake or two during the week. Like I said, she's a totally different prospect to that husband of hers."

"Does Mr Jenkinson know his wife is friendly with you and your wife?"

"I think he has an inkling. Gillian tends to visit when she knows he's out and not likely to return for hours."

"Seems odd to live a life of deceit like that, don't you think?"

"Deceit? I wouldn't quite call it that. She calls it 'evading the truth'. What he doesn't know can't hurt him, eh?"

"And what would likely happen if Mr Jenkinson was suddenly made aware of what was going on behind his back?"

"How should I know? He's a weird one. No telling what goes on in that thick head of his. Law unto himself most of the time."

"In what sense?" Sara asked. She peered over his shoulder to see if the kettle was boiling yet. It was.

He took the hint and stood to tend to his duties. "White, one sugar it was, wasn't it?"

"That's right."

He didn't respond to her question until he was back at the table. He reached for the biscuit barrel and offered them both a chocolate digestive.

They were Sara's favourite, and the temptation was too much for her to decline. "Thanks, I shouldn't but…"

Carla declined the offer, making Sara feel a lot worse as she nibbled through the chocolate.

"In what sense is Mr Jenkinson weird?" Sara repeated.

"In every sense possible. Hasn't got a good word to say about anything or anyone, that man. Drives me to distraction every time I lay eyes on the blasted bloke. I just know there's trouble brewing when he's in the vicinity."

"And do you retaliate at all, Andy?"

"I try not to. It's as though he goes out of his way to wind me up, though. A right bastard at times, he is."

"Have you had any interaction with him lately?"

"No, I try my best to avoid him whenever and wherever I can. If I see him setting off up to the top fields, I change my plans for the day and work on something on the lower ground or in the barns out the back."

"That's a shame. Especially as your paths are bound to cross now and again."

"It is. I've tried, believe me, over the years. He just doesn't want to know. He's content being wrapped up in his own insecure world. It's

Gillian I feel sorry for, she's the total opposite to him. She's a true member of the community, helps out at functions laid on by the church. She's a treasure in more ways than one. What on earth she sees in him…not my business, I know. Personally, I believe she deserves better."

Sara chewed her lip and then took a sip of her coffee as she decided whether to tell him about Gillian's death or not just yet. She placed her cup on the table. "I have some news for you, Andy."

"Oh, what's that then…? No, don't tell me, the price of beef has skyrocketed overnight." He rubbed his hands together and grinned at her.

Sara swallowed hard. "I can see you are a man who is always in good spirits. I'm afraid what I have to tell you is going to come as a shock to you."

"Sounds serious. Get on with it then."

"This morning, the loud bang you heard around an hour ago, was the Jenkinsons' car exploding."

"What? No way. Bloody hell, was anyone hurt?"

"Gillian was killed in the incident."

He shouted, "No!" and rose to his feet, tipping his chair back in the process. "What? I can't believe what I'm hearing. Are you sure it was her?"

"Absolutely sure, no doubt in anyone's mind, I'm afraid. Take a seat."

He scooped the chair up, flopped into it and placed his elbows on the table, nestled his chin into his palms and sat there, shaking his head from side to side. "How could this happen to such a beautiful soul?"

"It's our intention to find that out. The thing is, Mr Jenkinson pointed us in your direction."

"He did what? He thinks I have something to do with this? Well, that just shows you how warped that bloody man is. Why would I kill someone who I regard as a dear friend?"

"The problem is, Gillian was driving her husband's car when the explosion happened. So, from that, we're presuming the husband was the target and she was an unfortunate casualty in the proceedings."

"Jesus Christ. This is too unbelievable for words, and to think he's put me in the bloody frame for it. What an utter tosspot that man is." His hand moved to rest against his cheek. "I can't believe what I'm hearing. Gillian's gone! My wife, I need to ring my wife, she'll be gutted."

He reached for the phone, but Sara placed her hand over his.

"That can wait, Andy. We have more questions we need to ask you."

"Like what? I know nothing about this incident, I tell you. Why couldn't it have been an accident? Have you thought about that?"

"We have. It's too unbelievable to conceive such a thing, Andy. Mr Jenkinson told us that you're always falling out with him, is this true?"

"Yes, I've just told you that myself, haven't I?"

"You have. He also mentioned that someone has been sending him notes lately. Would you know anything about those?"

His frown deepened. "No. I can't believe this."

"What part?"

"Bloody all of it. Jesus, if that bastard is trying to frame me…I'll… I'll kill him."

"That kind of talk is only going to make matters worse."

"Tell me how I should react then, when you fling this type of accusation at me."

"Just be careful what you say, otherwise, as the leading SIO, I'm liable to misconstrue things."

"You can't be serious. That guy is the one with the warped mind, and yet here you are, badgering me. Tell me, do I have to answer your questions today? Because if not, then I'm going to ask you to bloody leave."

"No, if you'd rather answer our questions down at the station, that's fine by me."

"In other words, you have me by the short and curlies. Let's get one thing straight, I haven't stepped foot on that imbecile's land for it must be nigh on two years. Does that make things clearer for you?"

"Thank you. Not at all? Not even to visit Gillian behind her husband's back?"

His eyes narrowed, and he leaned forward. "We have never had any secret liaisons, if that's what you're damn well suggesting. She was a kind friend to me and my wife. You know, the wife I adore and have been in love with since we were teenagers. The same wife I have never felt the need to cheat on because we have a solid relationship and we rarely argue."

"What about the notes? Can you tell me if you've ever sent Mr Jenkinson one?"

"Why would I do that?"

"It's just that Mr Jenkinson mentioned that he'd received several."

He sat back and laughed. "And you think I sent them. I'm getting the impression that I'm in the frame for a lot in connection with that damned man. I have news for you. Yes, I despised him but I thought of Gillian as a cherished friend of *ours*. That said, I live an extremely busy life here on the farm, in which I frequently do over a hundred hours a week of sometimes very strenuous work." He pointed at Sara. "You bloody tell me how I would be able to do that if I'm supposed to be in my office, writing confounded notes to someone I despise. Anyway, what type of notes would these be?"

"The threatening sort," Sara filled in the blanks for him.

"What the fuck! Now I know he has lost his mind. If I fall out with someone I tend to ignore them, like anyone else would. I would not go out of my way to send them threatening notes which no doubt could be traced back to me. Don't tell me you haven't thought about the DNA side of things here?"

"We have. That will be our next course of action, sir. Think of this as me giving you the chance to put things right before we waste weeks waiting for DNA results to come into our hands."

"There you go again, giving me the option of admitting I had some-thing to do with this. I didn't." His gaze lowered to the table, and he shuffled in his chair. "I couldn't have written them. I can't write. I left school at thirteen because of bullying, and my parents home-schooled me, not very well I might add."

"I'm sorry to hear that. Are you telling me you can't write at all? Not one single word?"

"That's right. I believe the correct terminology you're searching for is that I'm illiterate. Once my parents started schooling me, I was put to work on the farm, therefore, farming is all I know. Saying that, it's never done me any harm. I repeat, I adore my wife. She has been my rock all these years helping me by handling all the admin side on the farm, I rely on her heavily. Another reason why I wouldn't cheat on her. I'd be lost without her, in more ways than one. My whole business would go down the pan in a nanosecond if she found me romping in the hay with another woman, let alone my closest neighbour, who has sadly now departed."

"I see. Okay, let's move on from that. What about the slaughtered ewe that was found?"

"Am I supposed to know what you're talking about there?" He scratched the stubble on his square chin.

"Mr Jenkinson said he found a pregnant sheep nailed to a tree, her belly cut open and the foetus hanging out, a few months ago."

"You're kidding me. This is the first I'm hearing about it. I'm sure Gillian would have told either Olivia or me about something as distressing as that."

"Are you inferring that he possibly made it up?"

He held his upturned hands out in front of him. "That's for you to decide. Do you want me to ring my wife to corroborate it?"

"Would you? That'd be helpful, although it could just mean that Mr Jenkinson swore his wife to secrecy about the incident."

"True enough. I'll ring her all the same." He stood and collected his phone from the worktop close to the range cooker and punched in a number. "Hi, love. I know you're probably busy. Yes, I'm all right. Listen, I have some sad news for you. I'm going to put the phone on speaker as I have the police here with me."

"Jesus, Andy, you're scaring me. What in the hell are you talking about?" Olivia's muffled voice filtered through the tinny mobile.

"Hello, Mrs Brady. This is DI Sara Ramsey here. Sorry if we're putting you out at all by making this call. Something has come to our attention that needs an immediate answer. I hope you understand."

"Umm…hello, er, no, not really. With regards to what? Why are you there, with my husband? Has something happened?"

Sara pointed at her chest and mouthed to Andy 'Do you want me to tell her?'

He nodded and swept a shaking hand through his hair. "The inspector is going to tell you, love. Are you sitting down?"

The air appeared to whoosh out of her body as she sank into a chair on the other end. "I'm sitting. Have you had an accident, love, is that it?"

"Hush now. I'm fine. Just listen to what the inspector has to say. All right?"

"Okay. God, I'm shaking here. What on earth could this be about to bring the police to our door? Should I come home?"

"It's me again," Sara said. "No, there's no need for you to return, stay and care for your mother. We were called to an incident about an hour ago involving your neighbours, the Jenkinsons."

"Oh my, what about them? If that man has hurt her…"

"Listen, love, without interrupting," her husband butted in quickly.

"Sorry, okay, I'm listening."

Sara glanced at Carla and tilted her head. She got the impression that the wife at least knew more than her husband. "How close are you to Gillian?"

"Quite close. Why? I'm right, aren't I? He's hurt her, hasn't he? I knew he'd do something the second I was out of the way. I've seen it coming for months."

"Are you saying they have marital problems, Olivia?" Sara's interest notched up the scale.

"Sort of. He's a horrible man. Rules the roost with an iron bar most of the time. I've always felt sorry for Gillian and the kids. I told her to get out and find someone new while she was still young enough. She told me I was talking out of my arse. I could see the marriage was dead, though. See the love she once had for him had died just by looking in her eyes."

"Did she openly tell you the marriage was over or are you telling me that's your personal opinion?"

"She hinted at it. My belief is that she's staying with him because it's the simpler option than uprooting herself and the kids and leaving the farm. It's not like she has any relatives she can go to around here. She knows she's welcome to come and stay with us, but that would be a little too close to home, I think, for her to even consider."

Andy rolled his eyes and sighed. "Love, stop talking and listen to what the inspector has to say."

"There's no need to be rude, Andy. I was asked the question and responded to it. Why are you taking this attitude with me?"

Sara raised her hand, preventing Andy from replying to his now agitated wife. Not ideal for what Sara had to tell her. "Olivia, I have news that may shock you."

Olivia gasped. "Oh God," she murmured. "Oh God."

"Unfortunately, an explosion took place at the Jenkinsons' farm, and sadly, Gillian died in the explosion."

Olivia's horrified scream vibrated through the phone.

"Love, Olivia, are you all right? Don't do this. Calm down, please," Andy was quick to comfort his distraught wife.

"I can't believe it. How did this happen, Andy?"

Andy stared at Sara.

She raised a finger to tell him she'd rather do the talking from now on. "She was setting off in her husband's car to get her hair done, and the car blew up."

"How does a bloody car blow up?"

"Forensics will need to carry out a thorough examination of the vehicle to verify what actually caused the blast. I'm sorry to break the news to you like this over the phone. The thing is, Mr Jenkinson believed someone targeted him with the attack, and we came to ask your husband a few questions."

"What are you saying? That man is accusing my husband of doing this ghastly thing?"

"Maybe. Mr Jenkinson mentioned he'd fallen out with a few people, and your husband's name cropped up. Bearing in mind the severity of the crime, it would be remiss of me not to come here and get your husband's side of things."

"He's not capable of doing something as evil as that. What the hell do you take us for? We're gentle folks. Farmers trying to earn a bloody living, not sodding terrorists. Good Lord, that poor woman. Did she suffer?"

"Highly unlikely. I'm sorry, I didn't mean to cause you any further upset. As you can imagine, time is of the essence this early on in an investigation. Mr Jenkinson mentioned that he's been receiving threatening notes lately, were you aware of this? That's not an accusation, what I meant was, if Gillian had mentioned anything along these lines."

"She did tell me he'd received a note or two a few months ago. Told me that Danny had got the police involved but as usual nothing had come of it. Don't tell me this has something to do with Gillian's death?"

"It could well be. We're going to look into the notes he received and the complaint he lodged when we get back to the station. There was also an incident involving one of the ewes, I believe. Do you know anything about that?"

"What ewe?"

"That's what I said," Andy interrupted. "I don't recall a sheep being killed, do you?"

"Definitely not. Is that what Danny told you?"

"Yes, he told us that a pregnant ewe was cut open and the foetus was hanging out of her stomach. She was nailed to a tree."

Olivia gagged. "Oh God, I can't believe Gillian wouldn't have let me know about something as monstrous as that. Unless she decided not to tell me because she knows how squeamish I am where animals are concerned. Bloody hell, why would anyone take their anger out on an innocent animal? That's beyond me."

"It does seem a little over the top. Okay, that's all we need to know, unless there's anything else you'd like to add?"

"I can't think of anything. Should we be worried about this? What if someone is targeting all the farmers in the area and we're next?"

"I shouldn't think that's likely. However, maybe it would be best if you and your husband remain vigilant all the same. We're going to do our very best to find the culprit as quickly as possible."

"Good to hear. Andy, do you want me to come home sooner than we agreed?"

"No, everything is fine here, love. You make sure your mum is comfortable first. You decide when you come back home, all right?"

"Okay, darling. I'm shocked by the news about Gillian. Damn, what about the kids? What will happen to them, Inspector?"

"I take it Danny will look after the children. He told me there are no other relatives in the area."

"God, I feel sorry for the little mites. He hasn't got a clue how to feed and clothe the nippers, the childcare has always been down to Gillian. Maybe I should return, you know, to help out with the kids."

Andy shook his head. "No, you have other priorities. He'll have to knuckle down and cope."

"You're a hard man, Andy Brady. Think of the kids and their well-being in all of this. He'll be grieving, well, I should hope he would be."

"Don't worry. We'll check in on him and appoint a Family Liaison Officer to be with him if we see him struggling with the children. We're not in the habit of leaving victims' families high and dry with no help available to see them through their grief."

"Is he? Grieving?" Olivia asked. "Sorry, I shouldn't have asked. It's just that he's always come across as a harsh man, lacking in emotion. Maybe I'm guilty of reading him wrong over the years and it's my bitterness showing. I feel more sorry for the kids. Maybe I should come home after all, Andy."

"No, I insist you stay there with your mum, out of harm's way, should there be someone dangerous in the area, love."

"Gosh, don't say that. I won't be able to sleep at night now, knowing that you're alone there."

"Now you're being downright silly. I'll be fine. I'm sure the police will be doing regular checks on the area during the evening and throughout the night, to ensure nothing like this happens again, won't you?"

"We can certainly arrange it, if that would help, just until we catch the person responsible."

"Yes, please, do it," Olivia said.

"Okay, you have my word. Please, try not to worry, Olivia. Thank you for speaking with me today."

"You're welcome. Please, make sure justice is served if this wasn't an accident. Wait, why was Gillian even driving his car? She's got her own."

"Apparently it was in the garage being repaired."

"Damn, okay, I didn't know. Poor Gillian. What an age to die at. Thirty-eight is no age at all, is it?"

"You're right, she was very young. Thank you for your time. Wishing your mother a speedy recovery from her operation."

"Thank you. I should be home within a week, that's the plan anyway. I'll ring you this evening as usual, Andy. Keep your chin up."

"I will. Speak later. Love you."

"Me, too."

Andy tapped the End Call button and returned to his seat. "See, she didn't know about the ewe either. I find that strange. If something as grave as that happened on a farmer's land, sorry, but word would spread like wildfire, especially around these parts. It's a very close-knit community."

"Maybe they decided to keep the news to themselves rather than get folks worked up about it."

His nose wrinkled with distaste at the notion. "No way. Any form of rustling or damage to the livestock is circulated quickly so that the other members of the community take the appropriate action to keep their animals safe. Why wouldn't he have told us? What's the logic behind him keeping it a secret?"

"I'm at a loss to know why. I'll make sure I ask him the next time I see him. Before we leave, is there anyone else you can think of who has fallen out with the Jenkinsons lately?"

Andy fell silent for a few moments. All the while he sat there, shaking his head. "I can't think of anyone. No, that's wrong, I'm sure I could come up with a whole list of people given time, but would those people have the capabilities to kill? I very much doubt it. God, I still can't believe Gillian perished in that damn explosion. Such a beautiful soul, inside and out. Too bloody good for him, if you ask my opinion."

"Both you and your wife have alluded to their relationship. Do you believe it should be something we should delve into, or is it just the fact that you don't get on with him that's possibly clouding your judgement?"

"Probably the latter. He's always been curt when he speaks. Gillian was warm and friendly. Olivia and I quite often said she reminded us of Princess Diana. A gentle soul who only saw the best in people. I don't know, maybe it's a case of opposites attract. She seemed to love him. They had two kids, so she must have loved him. It's just him, his attitude, his outlook on life is always so down and miserable. Maybe he was different when they were alone, locked behind closed doors."

"Did you ever hear them arguing?"

"Not really. He had a tendency to shout at her if she did something he didn't agree with. She appeared to shrug it off as though it occurred all too often." He rubbed the back of his neck and twisted it until it clicked. "Sorry about that, a bale of straw landed on me in the barn the other day, and my neck hasn't been the same since."

"Sorry to hear that. Have you visited the doctor?"

Andy laughed. "No way. I'd only be wasting his time. You get used to that type of thing going on, it's part and parcel of manual labour working on a farm."

"I see. Okay, we'll leave you to it then. Here's my card if you should think of anything else we should know about."

"Thanks, I'll show you out. I have a dilemma now," he said, once they reached the front door.

"What's that?" Sara inclined her head to ask.

"Should I go round there, you know, make sure he's all right? Or leave him to get on with it?"

"Hard to say what would be for the best right now."

"Okay, I'll leave him alone."

"Thanks for speaking to us. We'll be in touch again if we have any further questions in the near future."

39

"Are you going to have a word with Frank Dobbs now?"

"Yes, that's our next stop. Please don't call him to warn him we're on our way."

"I wouldn't dream of it. Good luck to you both. I hope you find the answers you're seeking soon, for Gillian's sake."

Sara glanced back to wave at the man once she'd reached the car, but he'd already gone inside and closed the front door.

"Strange," she murmured.

"Him or the situation?" Carla said.

"Both. Get in and we'll have a quick conflab."

Seated in the car, Sara asked, "What do you make of it all?"

"Sounds like a scene from that *Neighbours from Hell* programme. Warring neighbours, and there's usually only one outcome."

"Never seen it, too much like real life to me. I prefer to watch programmes that lead me away from the traumas of everyday life. When you say one outcome, does it usually result in a death?"

"Not always, but yes, sometimes."

"Sounds a bit extreme."

"It is what it is. Either way, Jenkinson didn't come out of the conversation in a good light, did he?"

"I was thinking the same. If Andy didn't do it then someone did, but who?"

"It seems strange they should target a car."

"Hmm… It does indeed, when there are a number of barns or even the house for them to attack, why go to all that bother of zeroing in on the car? Wouldn't it take time to rig something up? Presuming we're talking about something intentional, that is. What if we're wrong and this turns out to be a simple accident?"

"I doubt if we'll get the answer to that question for days, maybe even weeks. The PM and forensic examinations aren't going to be your everyday type, are they?"

"That's true enough. Okay, let's keep digging for now until we can't dig any further."

"The other neighbour?"

Sara nodded, started the engine and drew away from the farmhouse. She glanced back in her rear-view mirror with a bunch of questions streaming through her mind.

Could what Andy has just told us be some kind of smokescreen? He clearly didn't like Jenkinson. He just doesn't seem the type to kill. Could he have been having an affair with Gillian? I doubt it, he seems happily married. Could anyone else have had an affair with Gillian? Or was she just an innocent bystander who got in the way? Or are we dealing with a simple accident here?

2

F rank Dobbs was older than the first two men they had questioned that morning. He was in his sixties. What hair he had left was a very light grey, his skin wrinkled and tanned, his hands gnarled with arthritis and ingrained with dirt. But he had a genuine air about him.

"Thanks for agreeing to see us, Mr Dobbs. I appreciate how busy you must be."

He waved the suggestion away. "I've always got time to help out the police. What's this about?"

"We have a few questions to ask regarding your neighbours, the Jenkinsons. Would you be willing to address them?"

"Of course I would. Come in."

He led the way into what Sara thought her mother would have called a parlour back in the day. The furniture reminded her of the type used in a care home to give comfort to the elderly in their later years.

"Take a seat. Can I get you a drink?"

"We're fine, thanks for asking."

The three of them sat in the individual chairs, Frank opposite Sara and Carla.

"So, what about the neighbours then?" he asked.

Did he deliberately not use their names or is that me overthinking things?

"How well do you know them?"

"Hmm…tough question. I'd say I know Gillian more than her husband."

"I see. Have you had much interaction with Danny?"

"If by interaction you mean sit-down conversations with the man, then I'd have to say *no*. If, on the other hand, you're asking if the man and I have anything in common, I would have to say *very little*."

"And yet you're both farmers."

He grunted. "Some of us treat it as a livelihood and there are others who play at it."

"And you're the former and he's the latter, is that it?"

He smiled. "You cotton on quickly, Inspector."

For a woman, eh?

"I like to think of myself as intuitive, Mr Dobbs, it goes with the job. You were telling us that you believe Danny plays at being a farmer. Can you enlighten us as to why you believe that?"

"You'll have to take my word for it. Real farmers are out there in all kinds of weather from daybreak to nightfall. He seems to be what I call a fair-weather farmer. Brings his flock in during the winter far too early—still, if he has money to waste on the surplus food that would cost him, who am I to interfere?"

"I take it you don't get on with him, would that be right?"

He stretched out his neck and stroked it. "Possibly. Like I said, I've had more conversations with Gillian over the years than him. She's very welcoming, can't do enough for you. Always got time to say hello and pass the time of day for five minutes. This farming lark can be a little lonely at times."

Again, the avoidance of uttering Danny's name.

"Do you live alone, Mr Dobbs?"

"I do. Sadly, my wife passed away from leukaemia when she was in her late forties, around fifteen years ago." His eyes watered with unshed tears. "I've missed her every day since she passed. Gillian seems to sense that. She bakes me a pie now and again. I think it's behind her husband's back. She's an absolute treasure. Very caring, and those kids idolise her. She brings them with her when she delivers the pies, and they're little angels, so well-behaved, most of the time you don't even know they're around. They like to pop over to play with the puppies when I have a litter of Border Collies. I breed them, you see, not as many as I used to. I have a superb line of working dogs. Known in the area for them, I am."

"How interesting. They must keep you very busy, Mr Dobbs."

"Why don't you call me Frank, love—sorry, Inspector? I suspect you've worked hard for that title of yours over the years."

Sara smiled. "I have. Do you have any puppies here at the moment?"

He narrowed his eyes and twisted his mouth. "Why? Are you in the market for a working dog? I don't give these puppies out to just anyone, you know. The prospective owners are vetted to within an inch of their lives. I take it very seriously. Too many dogs end up on the scrap heap for my liking."

"Glad to hear you're a responsible breeder, Frank."

"See, now, that's the thing, I don't class myself as a breeder, even though I am one. It's the reputation I can't stand. People who know me, who have bought pups from me in the past, they always return for another one. I only breed quality pups."

"Do they all succeed as working dogs?"

"Very few of them don't, however, they're never returned to me. By that time, the families would have fallen in love with them. Anyway, that's enough about me—believe me, I could prattle on for hours about the dogs. What brings you here today? No, don't tell me. I heard a loud bang a while back. Does your visit have anything to do with that? I'm inclined to think it has, otherwise, why would you be asking me questions about the Jenkinsons? I'm right, aren't I?"

"You are, sir. I'm sorry to have to inform you that the explosion you heard was Mr Jenkinson's car blowing up."

"What? That's incredible. Faulty transmission, was it? Oh God, I hope no one was hurt?"

Sara tutted. "Sorry, but yes, Mrs Jenkinson died in the explosion."

He bashed the arm of his chair several times, hard at first, and then he appeared to run out of steam. "No, no, no...tell me it's not true. Not Gillian."

"It's going to be several weeks before the pathologist and Forensics can give us the true nature of the explosion. In the meantime, it's up to us to try to form a picture of the family and any likely problems they had with outsiders."

"Hang on, are you telling me this was a deliberate act?"

"Cautiously, we have to look at both possibilities. Either it was an accident or a deliberate act of violence."

"I can't believe what I'm hearing. That poor young woman. What will happen to those children now?"

Sara tilted her head. "Sorry, I don't understand."

"Now she's gone, I doubt if he'll watch out for them, not as well as she would have. He's going to have to change things regarding the way he manages the farm. I'm sure he'll cope, though, we tend to when our backs are against the wall, right? I had to when my wife passed away." He shook his head for a long time before he spoke again. "I fear for them. He's always come across as being a bit offhand with the little ones. Those kids were Gillian's world. To me, he tolerated them, found them to be an inconvenience at times."

"I see. But I thought you said you barely knew the man?"

"I don't. What I've seen and heard of what he has to say to those kids, well...their mother will be turning in her grave before long."

Sara raised a finger. "Whoa! Are you telling us that he abuses the kids?"

"I don't want to cast aspersions, please don't quote me on this. I've never seen him hit them but I've heard him aim a torrent of unkind words at them when they're out of their mother's sight."

"Was Gillian aware of this?"

"No, I tried to tell her but didn't have the heart to interfere in their marriage. Thinking things over now, I'm aware of how wrong that was. Oh shit! What have I done?"

"It's okay, please don't upset yourself. I have to ask you to revisit the incidents in question. Can you recall what he said to his children?"

"It was mainly name-calling. At first the kids laughed. I think they were guilty of thinking their father was fooling around with them, but the novelty soon wore off and the tone of his voice changed. That's when they were reluctant to laugh with him. Vile man. He went down in my estimation the second I heard the names he was calling them."

"Sorry, I have to ask, what sort of names?"

"The vilest imaginable. Names I would never say to one of my enemies, not that I have any, of course."

"Can you give us a hint?" Sara turned to face Carla, her eyes widening with trepidation.

"I suppose some of the worst ones are retards, idiots, thick shits. Who would call their children any of those names and far more besides? Especially not at that bloody age."

"Someone who was possibly stressed perhaps. Are you aware that Mr Jenkinson has been receiving threats lately?"

"No. Who from?"

"We don't know but we intend to find out. There's also been an incident in which one of his ewes was killed. Do you know anything about that?"

"Good Lord, I hadn't heard." He wagged a finger. "Even if that's true, no decent man or farmer would take that kind of shit out on their kids, would they?"

"No, you're right, they shouldn't do that at all."

"I'm glad we're in agreement. This is all news to me. Horrible news that I'm finding hard to digest. I can't believe I'll never see Gillian's face around here again. One in a million that girl was."

"So we've heard from your other neighbour, Andy Brady."

"God, I bet he was shocked to hear the news. He and his wife were really close with Gillian. Jesus, at times like this I know we should all go round there to show some compassion, it's just…neither of us like the bloke."

"Andy said the same. Thinking about it, maybe it would be good if you forgot the problems you've all had in the past and show him support in his hour of need. News of his wife's passing hit him badly from what I could tell. His main concern was for his children."

"Really? You do surprise me. I'll ring Andy, see what he thinks about showing the guy some support. Danny's not the easiest of blokes to get along with, though."

"Maybe if the pair of you reach out it could be seen as an olive branch and calm the waters between the three of you."

"I'll discuss it with Andy. You've only just met the bloke, we've had to deal with him and his damn mood swings for bloody years. It hasn't been easy, I tell you, not in the slightest."

"I'm sure. But, in my opinion he's going to need to lean on someone for support over the coming weeks."

"What about his family, can't one of them come here and stay for a while to help out?"

"He hasn't got any."

Frank frowned. "Sounds a convenient thing to say, to me."

"What makes you say that?"

"I don't know. How many folks do you know, with no kin whatsoever, who they can call on in their hour of need?"

"Not many, that's true. It's what he told us barely an hour ago, however. Why would he lie to us?"

"I'm not saying he has. I just find it incredibly hard to believe, that's all."

"We'll delve into it once we're back at the station. Can you tell me if you've either seen anyone hanging around lately or if you've had any threats from anyone in the past few months?"

"Why would I be threatened? I get on with anyone and everyone bar Danny, there's no need for someone to threaten me. And no, I've not seen any strangers hanging around. I'd be straight on the phone to your lot if I had, not that you're likely to do anything."

"We do our best, sir."

"Not from what I hear. Not where farmers are concerned. I have friends in other counties who have suffered with different things taking place on their land. They always report it to the police, but nothing is ever done about it. We're treated as second-class citizens, all the bloody time. We bring money into the economy, we pay our taxes like everyone else, we have a right to be protected, but rural crimes are treated as an inconvenience."

"I'm sorry if that's been your experience in the past. I'm not making excuses, but we've suffered severe cuts to the force over the years. That means major crimes are prioritised more than ever before."

"We all have our crosses to bear in this life, I guess. I didn't mean to have a pop at you personally. It's a grievance between farmers that just isn't being taken seriously. Anyway, that's old news. What do you propose doing about Gillian? She needs justice."

"We'll do all we can to find out what happened to her, I promise you. Perhaps you can tell us if you know of anyone else in the area who has had problems with the Jenkinsons?"

"With him, you mean."

"All right, with Danny. Anything come to mind?"

"Not really. Andy and I have fallen out with him a number of times, but we tend to steer clear of him nowadays. He's getting worse as he gets older, believe me."

"In what way?"

"Every way conceivable."

Sara snorted. "That doesn't really tell me much, Frank, care to explain?"

"Not really. I forget what the last thing I fell out with him was about. Something and nothing, I suspect, it usually is. Gillian acted as a peacemaker between the lot of us. Now she's gone, I dread to think what's going to bloody happen."

"You think there are going to be reprisals? Bad feelings will surface between you?"

"I can guarantee it now that she's out of the way. Have you got a direct line I can use to reach you? Because I think I'll need someone on my side down at the station."

"Seriously? You're not blowing this all out of proportion?"

He placed a hand over his chest and stared at her. "Would I do such a thing?"

Sara noticed a glint in his eye. "Are you winding me up, Frank?"

He raised his hand and held his thumb and forefinger apart an inch.

"Maybe a little. Thinking ahead, trying to prevent trouble before it brews."

"Well, I will leave you one of my cards but I'm trusting you to only get in touch if it's a genuine emergency."

"Of course, you can trust me." He winked and chuckled.

Sara liked this man, it felt natural being in his company. "Danny mentioned something about a bit of land grabbing, can you tell us more?"

"Bollocks! Sorry, shouldn't swear in front of ladies. But he does talk out of his backside at times. Those bloody boundaries have been in place for years. I even got in touch with someone from the Land Registry. They were all set to come up here and measure up when Danny backed down. That's the thing with him, call him on something and he has a tendency to turn and run. All mouth and no trousers, my old mum used to say back in the day."

"So there was no truth in it?" Sara pushed on, unsure if she believed Frank on the subject, judging by his cheeky expression.

"None at all. Silly man. He's the type to make a fuss about the slightest thing. It wouldn't surprise me if he cursed me for infesting his land with bloody moles. He's got thousands of molehills up in the top fields."

"Why would he? Do you have adjoining land?"

"I have, and my fields are clear. Years of expensive maintenance has seen to that. I get a man in, so to speak."

"A mole catcher?"

"That's right. Sees the critters off good and proper, he does. Some people think all farmers do is care for their livestock, but there's far more to it than that. You have to keep the land fertile to feed the animals. Moles suck the bloody life out of it, they do. You have to get rid as soon as you realise you've got a problem. He's not the type. I see him out there some days, staring into the distance, surveying his land and shaking his head."

"Have you offered him any advice on the matter?"

"More than I dare do. I made that mistake once with regard to the animal husbandry he needs to take care of. The bugger grabbed me around the throat and told me to keep my mouth shut and warned me to keep my opinions to myself. Shaking, I was, after that incident. Never realised until that day what a vile temper he had on him. It was Gillian who dropped by to offer an apology. I brushed it off, told her I wouldn't talk to the man again but she was welcome in my home anytime. She seemed so sad. She was a trier, that one."

"Trier? In what respect?"

"Always trying to fit in with the community. Like mud and water, they were. What she ever saw in him is totally beyond me."

"Well, in fairness, they do say that opposites attract."

"Phooey! How can you possibly live with someone who thinks and does the opposite to you? That statement has never sat right with me, and believe me, I've heard it dozens of times over the years. Surely if a marriage is to work, or even survive, there has to be some form of communication between the partners?"

"I think you're right. I've never met anyone who was a total opposite to their partner. Anyway, back to the couple in question. Did you have any cause for concern with respect to their family?"

He contemplated for the merest of moments and shook his head. "Not as such. I felt sorry for her being lumbered with an uncaring, despicable character. And no, I don't think that's too harsh a description for him."

"Thanks for that. Is there anything else you can add?"

"Not that I can think of. You're going to leave me a card, aren't you? I'll think things over once my head has cleared and give you a call if anything comes to mind. Can you make a note in that little black book of yours that I have concerns for the children?"

"We'll do that. I'll see what we can do regarding the nature of your suspicions as well, once we're back at the station. I can't thank you enough for talking to us today, the conversation has been very insightful."

"I'm not gossipmongering, I can assure you. I'd hate for anything to happen to those nippers. I could never forgive myself if I kept my mouth shut and said nothing at all."

"We appreciate your honesty and haven't taken it as malice in the slightest."

The three of them rose from their seats. He saw them to the front door and waved them off after Sara handed him one of her cards.

"Wow! Danny sounds like a right ogre, doesn't he?" Carla noted on the walk back to the car.

"True enough. We need to start digging. Let's get back to the station and set the wheels in motion."

*W*hen they pulled into the car park, Sara was puzzled to see the chief standing by her vehicle.

"Hello, boss, everything all right?"

DCI Price pointed at her offside front wing. "Does it look like it?"

"Ouch! How did that happen?"

"Some dickhead jumped a bloody red light at fifty miles an hour, or that's what it seemed like to me. Smacked into me, spun the sodding car around so I ended up facing the other way. By the time I got out the bastard had legged it. I've just run his plate through the system, and guess what?"

"It's stolen," Sara filled in.

"Yep. Just my luck, eh? The insurance company are going to love me."

"It was hardly your fault if the guy jumped the lights."

Carol Price kicked out at her tyre and then hobbled. "Shit! That seemed a good idea at the time. Instead, it's made things a darn sight worse."

"Come on, let's go inside. I'll buy you a coffee. I need to go over a new case with you anyway."

"Deal. I wondered where you'd been. A murder case?"

"Unsure at present. I think it's going to prove to be a perplexing one. A suspicion is already forming on a relative that is tying my stomach into knots."

"Sounds intriguing."

They entered the station together.

Sara stopped off at the reception desk to speak to the duty sergeant. "Something has come to light that's niggling me, Jeff. The victim's husband from the callout we've just attended told me he raised a complaint with us a few months ago and nothing was done about it."

Jeff's brow furrowed. "Jenkinson, right?"

"That's the one. Can you dig out the file for me and get someone to bring it up to my office?"

"I'll do it myself, ma'am."

"Thanks." Smile omitted because she was pissed off with the situation, she raced up the stairs to the incident room.

Carla set down a cup in front of DCI Price.

"How are you feeling?" Sara asked.

"Tearful, upset, angry, mixed emotions that I'm struggling to work through right now."

"The coffee will help. Did you get a good description of the guy?"

The chief pulled a face and shook her head. "Pass. Next question."

Sara tutted. "Helpful."

"In my defence, I had other things to consider like getting my car out of a sticky situation, and myself come to that. I was in the middle of a busy road, holding other drivers up at the traffic lights, plus the idiot's wreck was blocking the other cars, causing mass mayhem. And no, that isn't an exaggeration."

"I can imagine. Are you physically all right? Should you be checked over by the duty doctor?"

"I'll be fine, apart from the bump on my head, no real damage done. Stop worrying about me, my feelings of ineptness have turned to anger now."

"That's usually the order of things. If you're sure?"

"I am. Now, tell me about the case you're working, anything to take my mind off my own problems for ten minutes while the caffeine works its way into my system."

"Okay. It's a sad case but also a rather puzzling one. Carla and I were called out to a farm after an explosion occurred. When we got there, we found the farmer's wife had died in the blaze; she was in the farmer's car when it exploded."

The rest of the team were all listening attentively. A couple of them shook their heads in disgust.

"How terrible. Was this an accident? Do cars tend to explode like that? I'm not mechanically minded, so don't shoot me for asking such an incompetent question." Carol Price sipped her drink then smiled.

"Not to my knowledge. Anyone else have any knowledge on the subject?"

Barry raised his hand. "I've heard of a few incidents over the years, but there always seems to be a warning sign with the car. Actually, the cars seemed to have burst into flames during a journey. Can't say I've heard of one bursting into flames from a cold start. Want me to do some research, see what I can find out?"

"If you would. It seems strange to me. Anyway, the husband was distraught. They have two young children, five and six. Luckily, they had already left the house. The husband had walked them to the bus stop."

"That's fortunate. So the husband was shaken up, right?" Carol asked.

"Yes, very shaken up to begin with. By the time I started asking questions, his mood changed and he became angry."

"With you or with the situation?"

"I'm inclined to think the latter. He mentioned that he'd been threatened in the last few months, had even registered a complaint with us and nothing was done about it."

As if on cue, the door opened, and Jeff walked into the room. He handed her the manila folder he was carrying and exited again.

"Thanks, Jeff," Sara called after him, perplexed that he hadn't said a word but then thinking the chief's presence might have had something to do with that.

"Is that the complaint he raised?" Carol held out her hand for the file.

Sara gave it to her and addressed the team once more. "He told us that he'd had several threatening notes delivered to his house, but they didn't bother him to that extent. He was rightly perturbed about someone slicing open one of his pregnant ewes and nailing her and the foetus to a tree."

Carol glanced up, her eyes widening with the news. "You're kidding! What fucking sick individual would do such a thing?"

"I'm presuming the same person who then returned to fiddle with the farmer's car. I can totally understand him being aggressive towards us, if his complaint wasn't deemed urgent enough to investigate. Speaking to his neighbours, I get the impression that rural crimes in the area are on the increase and yet are being ignored. Maybe you can delve into that for us, ma'am?"

Carol shrugged. "I'll get the facts and figures, take a look at the reports that have been filed over the past year and get back to you on it. I saw a clip on *Countryfile* the other day that reported certain areas had seen an increase. Never thought ours would be one of those areas. If it's true, then I'm going to need to throw extra resources at it, just because of the number of farms we have in the area. I'd hate for the farmers to feel we didn't take either them or their chosen career seriously. They bring a lot of money into our economy, and they have the right to be treated the same as those of us living in the city."

"I agree," Sara replied, thankful the chief was willing to do some research on her behalf.

"It says here that the notes were handed over to Forensics. Have you checked with them yet? Oops, okay, forget I said that, you probably haven't had the time."

"No, that's right. I need to chase it up once we're finished here. One thing I took from the meeting with Danny Jenkinson this morning, well, and the interviews we held with his two neighbours, Andy Brady and Frank Dobbs, is that Jenkinson doesn't appear to be well-liked by folks in the area, unlike his wife. Both the neighbours appeared to be very upset by her death, said she had a kind heart and will be sadly missed."

"That's a shame. Was it the family car that she was driving?" Carol looked up from the file.

"No, it was his car. So if it was a deliberate act, whoever did this missed their intended target."

"Damn! How can you be sure about that? Did she have a car of her own?"

"Yes, it's in the workshop being repaired. Craig, I want you to ring the garages in the area—sorry, I forgot to ask Danny which one they used for servicing their vehicles. Do some digging and see what the outcome of her service is, would you?"

Craig nodded. "I'll get on it now, boss."

"What are you thinking? That the guilty person might have tampered with her car as well?" Carol asked.

"Possibly. Danny mentioned something about her brakes. It would be negligent of us not to check that out."

"I agree. Does the farm have any cameras on site?"

Sara shook her head and glanced at Carla. "I didn't notice any, did you?"

"I can't say I did," Carla admitted.

"That would have made our lives so much easier."

Carol nodded thoughtfully. "If he wasn't well-liked, does that mean he's had several barnies with people? Do you have a list of grievances to go through?"

"We've spoken to his direct neighbours. Neither of the men liked him, however, I didn't get the impression they would intentionally go out of their way to cause the family any aggro, especially as they both thought a lot of the wife."

"Where does that leave you then?"

"Up the proverbial creek, paddling like fury, hoping that some small clue comes our way. The pathologist will have a job on her hands, and the SOCO team, come to that. I can't see us getting any results back for a good few weeks, which will hamper the investigation, something I detest, but it's out of our hands, unfortunately."

"To be expected if the woman was blown to pieces. I'll be sure to take that on board and remember not to jump up and down on your head if I think you're dragging your feet on this one."

Sara's eyes widened. "Thanks, nice to know you think enough of me to back off a little."

Carol grinned. "What else did you find out?"

"The neighbours said they hadn't had any problems, didn't even know about the ewe when I asked them how they felt about it. Which I thought was odd. Upon reflection, maybe Danny was embarrassed and asked his wife not to put it around."

"Maybe. Does the man have any family he can call on in the area?"

"Nope, no one. I wondered if I should appoint a Family Liaison Officer to stay with him for a while. He assured me it wouldn't be necessary, but I'm concerned for the kids. He wasn't in the best state of mind when we left him but there's a uniform there to help out for now."

"If you have doubts, then yes, I'd definitely go down that route. Saying that, their job isn't to care for the children in the absence of a mother. Ring them and ask their advice. I'm putting it out there that I think they'll turn you down."

"I'll give them a call for clarification. That's about as far as we've got in the few short hours since the incident occurred."

Carol finished off her coffee and rose from her seat. "Okay, we'd all better crack on. Keep me posted daily on this during the week if you would."

Sara pulled a face.

"Nothing personal," Carol said, "I'd just like to be informed and see how things run with it."

"If you insist."

After the chief left, Sara issued the rest of the team with instructions to get the investigation rolling. Jill and Christine said they'd work together to delve into the couple's personal finances et cetera.

Sara drifted into the office and settled down to take care of the paperwork still sitting on her desk. Her tummy rumbled. She glanced at her watch; it was almost lunchtime. *Bloody hell, where has the morning gone?*

She was in the process of contemplating whether to send one of the boys on a baker's run when her landline rang. "Hello, DI Sara Ramsey, how may I help?"

"Hello, there. I'm Reverend Pratt from the parish of Lindley. I asked to speak to the officer in charge of the Jenkinson case, is that you?"

"That's correct, sir. How can I help?"

"I just had to ring up and say how distraught I am at hearing the news of Gillian's passing. She was a good lady, helpful and had become an important member of our parish. I shall miss her."

"It's a tragic loss, I agree, from what I've heard from her neighbours. Did you know her well, Reverend?"

"Well enough to know that she was going through problems at home."

Sara sank back in her chair. "In what respect, sir?"

"I was counselling her. She had the notion running through her head that she wanted to leave her husband. It's my role within the church to try to do everything in my power to prevent marriages from breaking up. She's been to me in tears over the last few months."

"Has she? Any specific reason why their marriage didn't appear to be working out?"

"She felt suffocated, that's what she told me. Didn't have a life of her own. Wanted and deserved more out of life is how she put it the last time we spoke."

"Which was when, sir?"

"A few weeks ago. She said she'd had enough, was trying to get the funds together to make a fresh start elsewhere for herself and the kids."

"Did she give you any specific reason as to why she wanted to leave her husband?"

"She no longer loved him. Hated her life being tied to the farm. Detested the isolation and not interacting with people. Just everything about farm life."

"Was her husband aware of this?"

"Oh, yes, very aware. He told her to 'suck it up and get on with things' I think was the terminology he used at the time."

"Can I ask what your relationship with Danny has been like over the years?"

"I've rarely spoken to him. He's not one for attending the church, whereas Gillian came every Sunday and brought the little ones with her. Oh dear, they're going to miss their mother, she was everything to them."

"Do you know if the children are close to their father?"

"I'm not one for speaking ill of people but I think all the parenting appeared to be down to Gillian. He's always so busy on the farm. I suppose that's to be expected. What's going to happen to the children now is of great concern to me. As a community we'd all like to lend a hand, however, I believe he's likely to slam the door in our faces, he's that type. I don't mean to sound disparaging of the man, especially at a time like this."

"I appreciate your honesty, sir. I met him earlier and have to say that I have certain doubts of my own I need to deal with—that's between you and me, of course."

"My lips are sealed. He seems a complex individual, wrapped up in his own little world."

Sara found herself agreeing with him. "Were you aware of the threats he's received in the past few months?"

"Vaguely. Gillian mentioned them in passing but didn't really go into much detail. Were they bad?"

"I suppose any threat can be classed as bad in the right circumstances. We're in possession of the notes that were left for Danny, or should I say, Forensics are. He also told us about a vile incident regarding one of his pregnant ewes."

"Oh, I had no idea things were that bad. And there's me running the man down. Maybe the stress factor needs to come into consideration here, what do you think, Inspector?"

"I have to concur. It's obvious both of them were under severe stress. On the other hand, this is the first time I've heard that his wife had the intention of leaving him. It sheds a different light on things, shall we say?"

"I'm unsure whether he knew of her intention to leave him. I believe she was making plans behind her husband's back. I warned her to be upfront with him, I believe honesty truly is the best policy, but each situation has to be considered in its own right. Don't you agree?"

"I do. One rule doesn't apply to everyone, it never has. Do you know if the marriage was an abusive one?"

"Oh gosh, I don't think that. Maybe it was and she kept that side of things a secret from me. If only he'd treated her right. The lack of love and the fact she felt like a slave most of the time… well, what woman can put up with that way of life for long?"

"Indeed. It's sad. I've spoken to the neighbours on either side of their property, and they told me that she used to regularly bake for them, although that appears to have been done behind her husband's back as well, that tells me she had a kind heart."

"That woman had the purest of hearts. I shall miss her."

"I appreciate you calling me today. Was there a specific reason for you reaching out like this?"

"Not really. I just wanted to tell you that my door is open if you want to discuss anything that goes on in this parish."

Sara sat upright and frowned, thinking it was a strange thing for the reverend to say. "Thank you. You're most kind. Conversely, if you should hear any gossip concerning the couple from any of your parishioners, will you let me know?"

"Of course I will. Good luck with your investigation. Good day, Inspector."

"Thank you again for calling, Reverend Pratt."

Sara ended the call and contemplated the conversation.

Carla poked her head around the door a few minutes later and asked, "We're sorting out what to do for lunch…wait, is everything all right?"

"I think so. Yes, lunch sounds a fabulous idea, we can discuss what I've just learned over that. I fancy an egg mayo on brown. Here's my dosh." She reached into her bag beside her desk, but when she sat up again, Carla had already left the room.

"I owe you anyway," her partner shouted.

"Fine. Thank you." She spent the next ten minutes sifting through her post, not that her mind was on the task, it was too busy going over the call she'd received from the reverend.

Another ten minutes flew past, Carla called her name, and Sara left her desk to join the others.

She stopped off at the vending machine and bought everyone a coffee. Settling down, her sandwich in hand, she went over her call with the rest of the team.

"Interesting," Carla stated, her mouth full of tuna and mayonnaise.

"I thought the same. A dissatisfied wife and mother on the verge of leaving her husband. What does that tell us?"

"Two scenarios come to mind," Jill was the first to say in between chomping on her baguette that was depositing a handful of crumbs on her desk every time she bit into it.

"Go on," Sara encouraged.

"Either someone has a major grudge with Danny, it was his car she got blown up in, or..."

Sara raised an eyebrow and tilted her head. "No, you think he did it?"

Jill shrugged. "Why not? Stranger things have happened."

"True enough. Let's not jump the gun here, the man is grieving the loss of his wife. I know his manner has been a bit dubious up to now but I'd rather give him the benefit of the doubt so far. Everyone, we need to take into consideration the threat angle. Damn, I meant to have chased up Forensics. I'll do it after this. Head like a sieve after my holiday."

"Honeymoon," Carla corrected.

"How easily I forget." Sara smirked. "I also need to get on to the Liaison Department, too. I was somewhat distracted by the reverend's call and the way it got my mind working. I'm still not sure I'm prepared to put Danny in the frame for knocking his wife off, just yet, though."

"Something we need to bear in mind," Carla added.

"Craig, have you finished trying to locate the garage?"

"No good so far. Still going through the list. The ones in the imme-diate area said they no longer dealt with the man."

"Interesting. Did they say why?"

"Most of them have had arguments about him querying their bills. I've just started ringing around the garages in the neighbouring towns."

"Who knew there were that many garages out in the country?"

"It surprised me as well until I thought of all the machinery they use on farms."

"Granted, never thought of that. How are we doing with the background checks on the couple?"

"Nothing there, as far as we can see. Very little money in either account. Gillian has more; she appears to have been putting some money aside in a savings account," Jill replied.

"In readiness for leaving him, I shouldn't wonder. Any police record for either of them?"

"I've searched the database and found nothing," Barry replied.

"What a joy, sounds like another frustrating time ahead of us, guys. Keep digging, there must be something to spark this investigation."

The team finished their sandwiches while Carla joined Sara at the whiteboard. Sara picked up the marker pen and jotted down the tiny amount of information they'd gathered so far.

"Not looking good, is it?" Carla whispered.

"Not really, I wish we had more to go on. The truth is, the facts are eluding us at present. Here, make yourself useful, you finish this off for me while I make some calls."

Carla took the pen from her and stood back to let her pass. "Good luck."

"Thanks, I'm going to need it." Sara closed the office door and retook her seat behind her cluttered desk.

The first call she made was to the Family Liaison Department. She spoke to a Nadine Clarke who assured her that she would call Danny to make arrangements to visit him. Sara ended the call and let out a sigh of relief. It was the children she was worried about, fearing that Danny wouldn't be able to cope with two boisterous youngsters during his grieving process. She made a note to chase Nadine up the following day to hear what the outcome was.

Next, she rang Forensics to chase up the report on the notes Jeff had passed on to them. Frustratingly, she was told that no prints or

DNA had been found on any of the notes other than Jenkison's. So where did that leave them? She was still contemplating the answer when Carla entered the office a few minutes later.

"Take a seat." Sara pointed at the chair.

Carla flopped into it. "Any good?"

"No go on the notes, and an FLO is going to ring Danny, go round there if necessary. I'm at a loss what to do next. Any suggestions?"

"Don't go looking at me, I'm as lost as you are on this one. All the checks we're carrying out are coming back negative so far, which isn't helpful, is it?"

"True enough. We need some snippet to fall into our laps, and I just can't see it happening on this one. See how Craig is getting on, with chasing down the garage. They might hold the key, in more ways than one."

"Will do." Carla set off again and returned wearing a smile. "He's found it. The mechanic said the car's brake lines had been cut. Seems like a deliberate act. They towed the car in."

Sara placed a finger and thumb around her chin and frowned. "Does this mean the person targeted both of them in that case?"

Carla shrugged. "What else could it mean?"

"I'm not sure. The notes said 'your next'. Apart from the person being semi-illiterate, it could have been directed at either one of them. According to the file, there was no name written on the envelope, only the note found inside. On that note, I would put Andy in the frame, but blaming him doesn't ring true with me."

"Hmm... the perpetrator intentionally went after the wife and not the husband? Why?"

Sara heaved out a long breath that puffed out her cheeks. "Your guess is as good as mine." There was a knock at the door, interrupting their conversation. "Come in."

Marissa opened the door and popped her head in. "Sorry, boss, you're going to want to hear this."

"Sounds ominous. Go on, Marissa."

"There's been another murder."

3

*M*arissa gave Sara the information which made her head spin. "Shit, we'd better get out there, Carla."

They raced through the station and jumped in Sara's car. She engaged the siren, as soon as they hit the main road, to help ease them through the traffic at that hour of the day.

"Shit, looks like there's been an accident." She weaved her way through and eventually found a clearing that would lead her back out to Northcott Farm.

This time the crime scene was on a neighbouring farm, at Frank Dobbs' residence.

She spotted Lorraine crouching next to Frank's body.

"Fuck, how the hell did this happen?" Sara asked, sudden tears pricking her eyes. She'd liked this man and was sad at his passing.

"The postman found him. He called at Northcott Farm just before he came here, saw us still attending the scene and came back to tell us. Poor bloke was shaking. He's sitting in his van over there."

"Okay, I'll get to him in a sec. How did the victim die, Lorraine? This is unbelievable."

"Isn't it? He was shot. I was in the process of wrapping things up at the neighbouring farm when I thought I heard a gun go off. I truly didn't think anything of it, what with us being out in the country, farmers shoot things all the time, don't they? It wasn't until the postie came back that things slotted into place."

"Damn. Maybe there's more to this than meets the eye. Someone took a risk of being caught, firstly, killing him in broad daylight, and secondly, knowing that the police and you guys were still next door."

"You're presuming they knew that," Carla chipped in.

"True enough. Bloody hell. He was a lovely man. He didn't deserve to die," Sara said, a stray tear slipping onto her cheek.

"Are you all right?" Lorraine asked, staring at her.

"I'll be fine. Frustration talking. Feel I've let the man down by not protecting him."

"You couldn't have known this was going to happen. How could you have predicted something of this magnitude, Sara? You're being too hard on yourself."

"Shit! What about Andy? We need to get him protection and quickly. Carla, go over there, call for a squad car to meet you. Whether he wants protecting or not, he's going to get it."

"On my way."

Sara threw her the keys to her car. "Be gentle with her."

"Of course."

Sara watched her leave, torn whether to remain by Lorraine's side or to seek out the postman to find out what he had to say.

As if reading her mind, Lorraine pushed her towards the post van. "Go and deal with him, he has his rounds to do. The victim isn't going anywhere, not for a while yet."

"I'm in shock. I failed him."

Lorraine grabbed both of Sara's upper arms and shook her head. "Now you're just being plain ridiculous. There's no way you could have foreseen this happening. Blaming yourself is wrong, Sara. Do I have to tell you to get a grip?"

"No. I'll snap out of it. Does Danny know?"

"No. I took off without checking on him. He's still in the house."

"Good. Jesus, who could be bloody responsible for this, Lorraine? None of it makes any sense to me."

"That's because we haven't found any clues to go on as yet. Keep the faith, Sara. Don't give up just yet."

"I have no intention of giving up, it's not in my remit."

"Glad to hear it. Go and talk to him."

Sara fished her notebook out of her pocket and crossed the gravelled driveway to the young postman who was staring out of his windscreen.

She knocked on the window and startled him.

His hand flattened against his chest, and he pushed open the door. "You scared the crap out of me."

Sara smiled. "Sorry about that. DI Sara Ramsey, I'm the officer in charge of the case. What's your name?"

"Pat Adams. Patrick Adams, sorry."

"That's okay, can I call you Pat? Oh my, you're not the notorious Postman Pat, are you?"

He rolled his eyes. "I never thought about it when I applied for the job. I've never seen a dead body before. It's shaken me up."

"I quite understand. I'll try not to keep you too long. I just need to find out what you can tell me about discovering Mr Dobbs' body."

"I'll do my best. Can I get out? I'm feeling hot and stuffy in the van and could do with some fresh air."

"Step out. Please, try and relax. In your own time, tell me what you saw."

He exited the vehicle, closed the door and leaned against it, his arms crossed over his slim chest. "I pulled into the drive as usual and found him like that."

"Was there anyone else around? Did you pass any cars in the lane on the way here?"

"No, not that I can remember. He was just there. The guys back at work aren't going to believe this."

"About that. I know it's going to be difficult but I'm going to have to ask you to keep quiet about it until we've informed his relatives."

"Oh, yeah, never thought about that. I can tell my boss, though, right? Otherwise he's going to be after my bloody knackers for being late with my other deliveries. He has us on a tight rein."

"Sorry to hear that. Of course, tell your boss with an added warning for him not to put it around, for now, anyway. Did you know Mr Dobbs?"

"Only a little. Nice man, always gave me a tip at Christmas, either money or a bottle of whisky. There aren't many folks who take the trouble to send a card around here, let alone give me a present, not that I expect it, of course."

Sara smiled. The man was acting nervously. She didn't find this strange, it was a common occurrence in the circumstances, when a dead body had been discovered.

"That was nice of him. Do you know if he had any relatives in the area?"

"A niece over in Hereford, I believe. Yes, she came to visit him last Christmas, if I recall rightly."

"I don't suppose you can remember her name?"

"Let me think. I should be good with names, shouldn't I?" His expression twisted in different directions as he thought. "Don't quote me on this, but I believe it's either Sadie or Sadia. Maybe Sadie, oh, I don't know."

"Don't worry, I'm sure we'll find her. Have you been on this round long?"

"Around seven years, I think."

"So you've got to know all the people in this area, I take it?"

"As much as any postie can. Why do you ask?"

"You're aware of what happened at the next farm, right?"

"Yes, very sad incident. Fancy two crimes as bad as that happening within the space of a few hours. This is usually a quiet community. You know, quiet, as in nothing really occurs, but to be confronted by two crimes of this nature, well, makes you shudder, doesn't it?"

"It's not good. Anything you can tell us will help immensely. At present we've got very little to go on."

His mouth dropped at the sides. "I can't help you, I'm afraid. Nothing bad is coming to mind. I think you'd be better off speaking to some of the neighbours."

"Yep, we're in the process of doing just that. I don't want to hold you up any more than is necessary. Take one of my cards. Will you ring me if you happen to hear anything I should know about on your rounds?"

"Anything you should know about? To do with what? I hear plenty." He smirked.

Sara raised an eyebrow. "I meant to do with the two crimes which have occurred today."

"Ah, yes, okay, sorry about that. I'll be sure to ring you, should anything crop up."

"Thanks for your time. I hope your boss goes easy on you."

He waved the card she'd given him. "I'll send him in your direction if he gives me grief."

"You do that."

Sara backed away to allow him to slip into his vehicle again and watched him drive away. She walked back to Lorraine who was down on her haunches, examining the corpse.

"You think he was shot here? In this spot?" Sara asked.

"I think so, no sign of a weapon. Anything from the postie?"

"Not really, very disappointing conversation with him. I think he was more concerned about what his boss was going to do with him for being late on his rounds."

"Jesus! Did he say that? Even though there's a frigging dead bloke lying within a few feet of him? Does a life mean nothing nowadays?"

"So it would appear." Sara glanced around. "The front door is open. Has SOCO been inside?"

"They're in there now. Do you want to take a look?"

"You read my mind. I'll just slip on a suit. Carla and I were only here a few hours ago, it would be good to see if the house is in the same state it was in earlier."

"Good idea. Looks like rain. I'm going to crack on, if you don't mind?"

"Go for it. Can I pinch a suit?"

"Sure, in the back of my van."

Sara stepped into the suit and attached the shoe coverings when she was standing on the doorstep of the farmhouse. "Anyone here?" she called out.

"Out here, in the kitchen," a man's voice filtered through the hallway.

Sara entered the room to find two technicians marking up the area. "What have you found, anything?"

"Droplets of blood. We've yet to discover who they belong to."

"Interesting, and yet Lorraine reckons he was shot outside."

"Exactly."

"Have you checked the rest of the house? What about the barns? He bred dogs."

"Only downstairs, we'll be moving upstairs in a tick. I'll get someone to check the barns."

"Mind if I take a look?" Sara pointed at the ceiling.

"No problem. You got gloves?" the younger tech asked.

Sara snapped a pair in place. "Always prepared. I'll be back."

The stairs creaked under her weight as she ascended them one tread at a time. The farmhouse was old, and she wondered how many interesting stories it held within its confines. The wallpaper dated back to the sixties from what she could tell. Her grandmother's hallway used to be decorated in a similar pattern, must have been all the rage back then.

She passed the tiny bathroom with its lemon suite and water-stained taps and across the landing into what appeared to be the main bedroom which overlooked the front of the property. The sheet and blankets were pulled back as if Dobbs was airing the bed, something the older generation tended to do more often than hers. The room smelt musty. The wardrobe dated back to the forties era with its stepped marquetry in each of its top corners. The closer Sara got to it, the more she realised where the smell was coming from.

Tucked alongside the wardrobe was a large safe. The door was open. She got down on the floor and peered inside. There were a few boxes of gun cartridges but no money. Did that mean someone had stolen it or wasn't there any to begin with? Why was it open? Had Frank come up here to retrieve the cartridges, thinking there was an intruder on his land? Or had the killer forced him to open the safe, removed the contents, then forced Frank back downstairs? Had Frank then tried to make a run for it and that's when the killer shot him?

Another couple of scenarios ran through her mind, but she decided to stick with the first two as they seemed more viable options. Either way, it had resulted in the poor man's death. Sara stood and looked out of the window. She had the perfect view for miles around, the Malvern Hills off in the distance and field upon field in between. To the right she could just make out Northcott Farm, and down the road on the left was Wyle Farm where Andy Brady lived. Three farms within close proximity of each other, and yet two of the farmers hadn't got on well with Danny. That was the strangest part in all of this, and Sara couldn't help wondering if that was out of jealousy or whether it was a case of a clash of personalities.

She unzipped her suit and removed her mobile from her jacket pocket. Staring out towards Andy's farm, she rang Carla. "Hi, just checking in with you. How are things there?"

"Fraught. Andy is pacing the floor. He's upset about Frank but also concerned that there's more going on here than any of us realise."

"Yep, I'm inclined to agree with him. Can you ask him how well he knew Frank?"

"Hang on, I'll ask. Any particular reason?"

"I've located a safe in Frank's bedroom, it's empty. I just wondered if he knew whether he kept any cash here."

"I'll check. Do you want me to get back to you?"

"No, I'll hold."

Carla asked Andy the question.

"He kept a bit of cash in the house, no idea how much, though," Carla relayed the answer.

"Okay, not helpful, but it'll have to do for now. Has the backup arrived yet?"

"I've just heard from them, they're five minutes away. Want me to come back there?"

"Give it five or ten minutes then yes, rejoin me, if you would."

"Okay. You sound subdued, everything all right?"

"Apart from having two murder cases to deal with on the same day, yep, everything is just dandy."

"Sorry, poor choice of words. I'll go now."

"Hey, I wasn't having a pop at you. I'm fine, lost in thought as usual. See you soon." Sara replaced her phone, zipped up her protective suit once more and went back downstairs. En route, she poked her head into the other three bedrooms. Two of them were filled with boxes, and the small one at the top of the stairs turned out to be an office and contained a desk and filing cabinet but very little else. On the far side of the desk was a spike full of receipts and a *Simplex D* accounts book in the centre, sitting on the inlaid leather.

From an outsider's point of view, everything had a place in Frank's house. She wandered into the lounge and spotted a shotgun standing up against the wall behind the floor-to-ceiling flowered curtains.

"Boys, you might want to come in here."

Both the techs appeared in the doorway, seemingly perplexed by her summons. That was until Sara drew back the curtain and pointed at the gun.

"Jesus! How did we miss that?" the older man asked.

"Easily done with the curtains drawn," Sara replied, smiling.

"I'll get it dusted for prints." The younger man dipped back into the kitchen and reappeared carrying a silver case. He placed it on the floor close to the gun and extracted a camera. He fired off several shots, put a marker on the wall, windowsill and floor then lifted the gun in his gloved hand and dusted it. He glanced at Sara and smiled. "We have something."

"Good, let's hope it belongs to the killer and not the victim. I have a feeling it's going to be the latter as I think it's probably his gun."

"We'll soon see."

"I'll let Lorraine know, I'm going back outside anyway." She nodded a goodbye and left the house.

Lorraine looked her way, and they locked gazes.

"I found a shotgun inside, it's probably the murder weapon."

"You found it?" Lorraine frowned.

"Yep, it was standing up behind the curtains in the lounge. I should have noticed it sooner, like when I walked into the house."

Lorraine tutted. "The techs should have, you mean."

"Whatever. It's been discovered. I also located a safe upstairs with cartridges inside and nothing else."

"No money?"

"Nope, so it might well have been a robbery."

"They took the cash, killed him and left the weapon here waiting to be found?"

"Hmm…that does sound bizarre. Who knows? Carla's on her way back. I'm not sure where to go next."

"Will you be canvassing the other farms in the area?"

"Yep, I'm going to get a squad of people out here. Two fatal incidents in one day is…well, inconceivable. Apart from showing up in force, I'm really not sure what else I can do."

"True enough. Hey, don't you dare go blaming yourself for this, Sara Ramsey, be kind to yourself. Having second doubts or going on a downer isn't going to catch the bastard responsible, is it?"

"I know." She heaved out a breath and pulled her shoulders back, straightening her spine. She glanced down at Frank's body and shook her head. "He didn't deserve this. I know I only met him the once, but he was a nice man, I could tell. How many shots?"

"Sorry to hear that. There's just no justice for some folks in this life. Two shots, one to the chest and one in the head."

"Why?"

Lorraine sighed. "To make doubly sure he was dead, I suppose."

"One shot would have been enough to have killed him, though, right?"

"I know that look. What are you thinking?"

"It was personal and not a stranger chancing his arm perhaps."

"Possibly. Let's see what we can gather in the way of DNA to put that theory to the test."

"I hate to ask and appreciate you have a lot on your plate but…"

"You want me to give this case priority, yes?"

"Well, only because the victim is in one piece and not in thousands of pieces like Gillian Jenkinson."

"Hardly, but I get what you mean. Okay, I'll do it, just this once."

"Fantastic. Here's Carla now." Sara marched across the drive to where her partner had parked the car and opened the driver's door. "How did it go?"

"He was shaken up. Devastated to have 'lost two good people in one day' was how he put it."

"It is a shocker. He's being watched over now, though, isn't he?"

"Yep, two PCs showed up. I've told them not to move from outside the house. Anything suspicious they need to report to us ASAP."

"Good. We've found a possible weapon. Lorraine is going to have a word, see if Forensics will prioritise the DNA tests for us."

"Let's hope the results come back with something. Do you think we should check in on Danny, make him aware of what's happened?"

"Yes, let's do that. I'll just see if Lorraine has anything else for me before we head over there." She trotted back to see her pathologist friend. "If you don't need me, we're going to drop back to see Danny."

"No, you go ahead. My guys are finishing up over there, or they should be."

"See you later." Sara stripped off her protective clothing and disposed of it the usual way, placing it in a black sack near to Lorraine's vehicle, then joined Carla back at the car.

Carla went to get out of the car.

"No, stay there, you can drive for a change."

"If you're sure. What do you think is going on?"

"Fucked if I know at this point. Someone with a vendetta perhaps. Why would two neighbours be killed within hours of each other?"

"Makes you wonder. Maybe the reverend can tell us more, or perhaps the local shop or landlord of the pub, especially if it's a close community."

"Good thinking. Let's do this first, not that I'm looking forward to seeing him again so soon."

"May I ask why?"

"I get the impression he's the type who is going to be on the phone every five minutes, demanding to know what we're doing about solving his wife's murder. While that's understandable, it can also be a hindrance."

"True enough."

Carla indicated and pulled into Northcott Farm. The PC was standing outside the house. She seemed down in the mouth.

"Everything all right?" Sara asked.

"I hate to tell tales, ma'am, but the sooner I'm out of here the better."

"Why? What's happened?"

"Not long after you left, he had a right go at me. Told me the last thing he wanted was 'us lot' spying on him and to bugger off. I told him I was only following orders and I had to stay as we only had his safety in mind. He told me to wait out here. Which suits me."

"I'm sorry you were spoken to like that. Maybe we should make an exception for him, perhaps it was the grief talking."

"Maybe, ma'am."

Sara smiled at the PC and gestured for Carla to enter the house. They walked into the kitchen to find Danny sitting with his head bowed at the table.

"Hello, Danny." Sara glanced around the room, already feeling uncomfortable in his presence. She wasn't looking forward to sharing the news and had the feeling a backlash was coming her way, especially after what the PC had just told her.

"You're back. Why? To badger me some more?"

"Nothing could be further from the truth. Sorry if you think that's what I was doing the last time I was here. I was only doing my job, trying to figure out who was responsible. We have some news for you."

His head shot up, and his steely grey eyes met hers. "You've found the culprit?"

"No, sorry. We've just come from Frank Dobbs' farm."

"Oh, him! I bet he told you all sorts of bloody lies about me, didn't he?"

"Actually, it was our second visit there today. During our first visit earlier, we questioned him, tackled him about the problems you raised between you, but he shrugged them off. Didn't really think much of them, if you will. Then we headed back to the station where I brought my team up to date with the investigation. We received a call around half an hour ago to attend Frank's farm again…"

"What are you saying? Do I really want to hear all this shit? How you go about your day? I'm grieving the loss of my wife here, get on with what you have to tell me and get out."

"Okay, I have some more bad news for you in that case. Frank Dobbs is dead."

His head inched forward, and he stared at her. "Dead? What do you mean? How did he die? Was it a heart attack or something?"

"No, unfortunately, he was murdered."

Danny stood and tipped his chair over in his haste to get to his feet. "What the fuck? How? None of this is making any sense."

"He was shot twice with his own weapon it would appear. Didn't you hear the shots?"

"Of course I didn't, why would I?"

"It's just that the pathologist who attended the crime scene here heard them."

"Good for her. I've been inside the house since you left. That's too bad for the old sod. What are you going to do about this? Two murders in one day."

"Well, we've yet to establish how your wife died, it could have been an accident. We'll know more once the results from the PM are back."

"And you expect me to believe that after hearing that old Frank has now copped it as well? Are you just out of Hendon, Inspector? Surely even an inexperienced copper would be able to piece this case together by now."

Sara's cheeks warmed. *How dare you!* "No, for your information, I've been in the force a fair few years, Mr Jenkinson. My job is to collate all the evidence and investigate a crime thoroughly. There are procedures we need to adhere to if we intend for a case to go to court, something that needs to happen to put a suspect behind bars. Considering the time in between the incident with your wife happening, around nine this morning, and the fact that it is only…" She paused to look at her watch. "Just gone one-thirty now, I don't think we're doing too badly, I have to say."

"Whatever. I think you're somewhat deluded, given you have yet another *murder* case on your hands. When are you going to realise that someone has it in for me? I've handed you the proof of the notes, you're going to have to take my word about the ewe that was killed. Sorry I didn't think to take a photo of the sickening crime at the time. Them's the breaks, eh?"

"I take what you're saying on board. The first thing I did when I returned to the station was source your complaint. I then rang Forensics to see if they'd had any joy, and no, there was no DNA found on the notes. Which, as you can imagine, becomes a stumbling block for any officer trying to solve a crime."

He snorted and shook his head. "You really think someone as vindictive as this wouldn't think to cover his back? You don't have to be Einstein to know how DNA works these days, it's all over the TV and in the newspapers."

"I agree, which also makes our job that much harder in the long run. I can assure you, given the time frame we've had to deal with the crimes that have been committed today, I think we're doing an excellent job so far."

"So, by that statement, are you telling me you have someone in mind?"

"Not yet, no."

He let out a derisory laugh. "You're unbelievable. If you think you can fool me with your gibberish, you've got another think coming. You should go before I say something I'm likely to regret. I'm sorry to hear about Frank, but that's as far as I can go, bearing in mind I'm grieving the bloody loss of my wife. Have some respect, Inspector. Leave me to grieve without showing up on my doorstep to hound me every five minutes with other crimes that have been committed in the damned community. I don't want to know about them. I have enough on my ruddy plate as it is."

"I'm sorry you feel that way. All I was doing was making you aware of what other crime had been committed on your doorstep, and also to tell you that we'll be linking the crimes. The last thing I wanted to do was come here and cause you any further upset, so please forgive me if I've ended up doing just that."

"You've said your bit, now, if you don't mind, I'd like to be left alone to grieve. I need to get my head around how I'm going to tell my kids that their mother died this morning."

"I've always found honesty is the best policy, sir."

He laughed again. "Okay, so, if my five- and six-year-olds have a meltdown I'll send them in your direction for consolation, shall I? Go on, get out and take your useless advice with you, for fuck's sake. And yes, I'll be ringing your superior to make a complaint about you."

"That's your prerogative, Mr Jenkinson. I think you'll find that up until now, I've conducted myself according to the procedures we have in place."

"Is that right? Go, I've had my share of useless coppers being around me today. I gave you evidence months ago, and your lot chose to ignore it. None of this would have happened if I'd been taken seriously at the time. You'll have to forgive me if I don't take what you, or any other police officer has to say seriously."

"I understand how angry you must be feeling right now, sir, all I'm asking is that you give us a chance."

"You'll get your chance but on my terms. If I want you off the case then I'll make sure I get my wish."

Sara shook her head. "Sorry, it doesn't work that way."

"What are you saying? That I'm stuck with an incompetent frigging female detective whether I like it or not?"

"I'm the appointed SIO on your case, sir, yes, you're stuck with me. For your information, I have an exemplary record in solving crimes in this area."

"Serious crimes?"

"Very serious crimes."

"They must have been dumb criminals for you to have caught them, that's all I'm saying on the matter. Goodbye, Inspector."

"Have it your way, Mr Jenkinson. I appreciate you're dealing with your grief at the moment, but I just want to reiterate that you'll have my word that we'll give it our all to find the culprit of the two crimes." She was tempted to add 'enjoy your day' at the end but didn't deem it appropriate in the circumstances.

Sara and Carla left the farmhouse.

Sara let out an exasperated breath the second she stepped outside the front door. "Sometimes, just sometimes, I have a desire to punch folks' lights out. This is one of those times."

"I wouldn't blame you either. The gall of the bloody man. Maybe he's got a downer on women."

Sara nodded. "I'm getting that impression, too."

A car pulled into the drive, and a young brunette woman got out. She dipped into the back seat of her car and withdrew a briefcase. At the cordon, she showed some form of ID to the constable who raised the tape for her. Sara smiled at the woman walking towards her.

"Hi, I'm DI Sara Ramsey, the SIO working the case. Can I ask who you are?"

The woman held out her slim hand for Sara to shake. "Annabelle Holmes, I'm the new Family Liaison Officer for this area. I've come to offer my support to Mr Jenkinson. Is he inside?"

"He is. I'd introduce you, but he's just sent us packing. Good luck, I think you're going to need it."

"Ouch! Thanks for the warning. He must be confused right now, what with losing his wife this morning. Such a tragic case."

"It is. We've just come from a neighbouring farm where the farmer was found dead as well. If you stay, please be aware that you might be in danger."

Her eyes widened. "Okay, not what I was expecting to hear, but thanks for the warning. Is he inside?"

"Yes, in the kitchen." Sara and Carla took a step to the side to allow the woman to ring the bell. "We'll be off. Here's my card if you need me at all."

Annabelle slipped the card into her jacket and smiled. "Thanks, I appreciate it. Let's see what sort of reception I get."

Sara and Carla walked away. They reached the car but turned when they heard Danny hurling a verbal attack at Annabelle.

Carla blew out a breath. "Shit! What is wrong with that fucking man, doesn't he understand all we're trying to do is help him?"

"I think the concept is lost on him. Christ, she's in tears. I'm going to have to step in. Bastard." Sara stormed back to the farmhouse, her hand raised in front of her. "Mr Jenkinson, go back inside. Annabelle is here to help you. You have no right speaking to her this way."

"She's on my frigging property. I told you I didn't need an FLO or whatever she's called. Get her out of here. Now."

Annabelle turned to face Sara. She seemed bewildered and extremely upset by his abusive tongue. "I was only trying to help," she muttered.

"Take your pitying sympathy elsewhere, I neither need it nor want it. Got that?" He slammed the front door and attached the chain to it.

Sara placed a comforting arm around the young woman's shoulders. "Come on. If he doesn't want our help then he's going to have to get on with things himself."

"All I did was introduce myself. I don't think I've ever been subjected to anything as bad as that before. I'm shocked."

"You need a nice cup of tea, love. Please don't take it personally, he'd just had a go at me. You turned up at the wrong time. It would be best if you left him alone for the rest of the day. Try calling him tomorrow, see if he's more willing to accept your kindness and help then."

"I'm not sure I want to return, not after what he's just dished out. What about the children? Do you think they're going to be safe with him?"

"Hard to say under the circumstances. He appears to have their best interests at heart. Only time will tell," she replied, pushing aside a niggling doubt.

"What an awful day this is for him. You'd think he would bite our hands off if all we're trying to do is help him, wouldn't you?"

"It's the grief rearing its ugly head. There's no telling how it will affect some people. Don't take it to heart. Thanks for trying to help him."

"I think I'll pop a card through his door, in case he changes his mind."

"Good idea. I'll do it for you." Sara took the card and shoved it through the letterbox. Within seconds, the card flew back out of the letterbox, and a loud thud sounded on the other side as if Jenkinson had thumped the front door. "It'll be best if we all leave him to it, if that's what he wants."

"Hallelujah!" Jenkinson shouted from his hallway, obviously overhearing her.

Sara guided the woman back to her car. "Will you be all right to drive?"

"I think so, although my knees are still knocking together. Why do people react that way when there's help on offer?"

"It's beyond me. Take care. Let me know if he gets in touch with you in the future."

"I will. Thank you. I'm glad you were here to assist me, I'm not sure how I would've coped if you hadn't been."

"All part of the service."

Annabelle slipped into her car, reversed and drove away.

Sara and Carla did the same, leaving Danny alone at the farmhouse except for the few remaining SOCO techs examining the car. On the way back to the main road, they passed a breakdown lorry.

"Probably going to pick up Danny's car," Sara said. "At least our guys will be off his property soon."

"That should please him. What next?"

"Back to base. We need to see if we can track down any of Frank's relatives. The postie seemed to think he had a niece called Sadia or Sadie, living in Hereford somewhere, we just need to find her."

"Want me to get in touch with Christine, see if she can locate her in the system?"

"Yes, okay. We can call in and see her, to break the news, before we head back to the station."

4

$\mathcal{C}$hristine instantly found what they were searching for. Sadie lived in a block of flats close to where Sara's brother used to live before his untimely death. She fell quiet.

Carla must have sensed what was running through Sara's mind because she asked, "Are you all right?"

"I think so. Mum's asked me to clear out Tim's flat, but I haven't got it in me to go back in there yet. Maybe my sister will come with me on Saturday or Sunday. The landlord is getting antsy, which is totally understandable on his part. He's losing money daily with the flat lying empty."

"Want me to give you a hand? It's not as if I'm doing anything else now that Gary and I have split up."

"Let's see how the investigation pans out first. We might have to pull in some overtime this weekend by the look of things."

"Ugh... I hope not. After Jenkinson's display back there, the less interaction we have with him the better."

"I'm with you on that one. We'll do our best to avoid him. It doesn't mean I'm willing to give up on his case, though. Both his wife and poor old Frank need justice for what's happened to them."

"I know," Carla admitted sullenly. "Life can be such a bitch at times."

"Yep! Can't say I'm looking forward to having this chat either."

Thankfully, Sadie's flat was only three flights up. Sara rang the bell.

A young woman with black hair and a friendly smile answered the door within seconds. "Hello, can I help?"

Sara and Carla flashed their IDs. The woman appeared taken aback momentarily before she recovered.

"DI Sara Ramsey, and this is my partner, DS Carla Jameson. Are you Sadie Dobbs?"

"That's right. What the hell is going on?"

"It would be better if we came in and spoke with you for a moment."

"About what?" Sadie clutched the door tighter.

"Your uncle."

"Uncle Frank? What's he been up to now?"

What did she mean by that? Was Frank usually 'up to something'? "Please, it would be better inside," Sara insisted.

The young woman finally relented and let them in. She showed them into a tiny box lounge which had minimal furniture and the smallest TV Sara had ever laid eyes on.

"Sorry, I don't have many chairs, or much furniture at all come to that. I'm just getting on my feet after leaving home for the first time. You have the chairs and I'll sit on the bean bag." She sank into the multicoloured bag and crossed her legs at the ankles.

Sara and Carla sat in the two IKEA-style, slightly padded chairs which turned out to be far more comfortable than they first appeared.

"Sorry, Miss Dobbs, it's not good news, I'm afraid. This morning your uncle was shot at his farm; he didn't survive."

"What? No way. How? Did his gun backfire or something? I told him he needed to be careful with that damn thing. Oh shit, what am I saying? That's not what you meant at all, is it?"

Sara shook her head. "Let me try to explain what we've been dealing with since first thing. We received a call to say there'd been an explosion at a neighbouring farm. When we arrived, we found the lady of the house had perished in a fire—the farmer's car had gone up in flames. An hour or so later, we called on Frank to get his take on things as the farmer, Danny Jenkinson, had pointed a finger in his neighbours' direction."

Sadie raised a hand and shook her head. "Sorry, I'm finding it hard to take all of this in. Jesus, Uncle Frank is dead...but he can't be. We were very close, he was like a second father to me. I lost my dad a couple of years ago to cancer, and ever since then Frank's kind of taken me under his wing."

"I'm so sorry for your loss. He seemed a very nice man."

"He was, he was the best. Which begs the question why someone would kill him? That is what you're telling me, isn't it?"

"It is. After questioning him this morning, we went back to the station to begin our investigation. We received the call from the local postman sometime after lunch to say that Frank had been shot twice."

"Why? Why would anyone want to kill him?" She covered her eyes with her hands and sobbed. "Oh God, this could bloody kill Mum after losing Dad. She's going to be heartbroken to hear this news. He was such a gentle man. I can't believe this."

"He appeared to be a decent sort when we spoke with him earlier. When was the last time you saw him?"

"At the weekend. Mum and I made a roast dinner for him at his place, it's what we always did, every Sunday." Her hand shook as she tucked her hair back from her colourless face. "How will I tell her? I doubt if I'll be able to say the words. Killed, you say? This is horrendous news. He was one of the sweetest men. I know I'm bound to say that being his relative, but he was. Hang on, what farm had the explosion?"

"Northcott Farm, the Jenkinsons' place."

"Oh heck, yes, you said, sorry, it didn't sink in. The wife is dead? Jesus, this is unbelievable. Frank thought the world of her. Gillian, wasn't it?"

"That's right. What can you tell us about her?"

"I met her once or twice. Long-suffering wife of that fecking idiot.

She should have left him years ago. Their kids are angels, but he's horrible. I remember one day when I was visiting Uncle Frank..." She paused to catch her breath. "Gillian had brought him an apple pie she'd made; the two kids were there, too. Anyway, the three of them were inside having a cup of tea with us when her husband showed up. He shouted at her to get out of Frank's house and go home. Poor Gillian gathered the children and shot out of the house. Uncle Frank was livid. He wanted to go after them, give Danny a piece of his mind, but Mum and I prevented him from doing it. That week they'd had a set-to about Danny accusing Frank of robbing some of his land. He's a bastard. If you could have seen the fear emanating from his wife. Shit! I can't believe both of them are gone."

"Interesting. Do you know if your uncle had fallen out with anyone else recently? Maybe in the past six months or so?"

She stared at the wall next to her as she thought. "I can't think of anyone. I know he was concerned about Gillian, the way her husband treated her. He adored the children, too. How has this happened? That they should die within a few hours of each other?"

"We believe that Danny might have been the target of the explosion because his wife was using his car. He mentioned that he'd been receiving threatening notes lately. I don't suppose you know anything about those, do you?"

Sadie's brow knitted together. "What are you saying? That possibly Uncle Frank had something to do with that?"

"No, I just wondered if Gillian might have mentioned it in passing, that's all."

"If she did, I can't remember, sorry. I've just thought, how will the children cope without their mother? From what I could tell, Danny didn't know how to handle them, not like other fathers do. What a bloody mess. What are you doing about it?"

"We're interviewing as many people as we can right now. Are you telling us that Danny was a reluctant father or an uncomfortable one?"

"Hard to pinpoint which. To my knowledge, I don't think he wanted kids in the first place. He was very possessive with Gillian's time from what I could see. Hence him storming over to Uncle Frank's and dragging them all back home. It was pitiful to see the change in her. One minute she was smiling, enjoying her time with us. Then the second she heard his voice at the front door her whole demeanour appeared to crumble before our very eyes. I'd never let a man treat me the way he treated her, not in a million years."

"Do you think she intended to leave him?"

She shook her head and shrugged. "I don't know, I wouldn't blame her if she did have those thoughts running through her head. He's a hateful man. Made my uncle's life hell on several different occasions. But Uncle Frank never held it against Gillian. If anything, it made his affections towards her come to the fore, if that makes sense?"

"It does. Do you think your uncle thought of himself as her protector?"

Sadie pointed and nodded. "I couldn't have put it better myself. Yes, that's exactly how I would define it. Uncle Frank thought more of women than men, let's put it that way."

"Sad that he's no longer with us."

"I'll miss him. I'm dreading breaking the news to Mum."

"Would you rather we did that? Is she local?"

"Yes, she lives in Bartestree. No, I think she would prefer to hear the news from me. I have the day off today, I'm due to go over there for dinner tonight. I'll tell her then. She's going to be distraught, the same as me. Do you think the same person targeted both of them?"

"It seems too much of a coincidence to think otherwise. That's why we need to know if your uncle had fallen out with anyone."

"You know what? I can't think of anything, apart from him arguing with Danny about the land issues and other niggly things to do with their boundaries. That man always seemed to be disrupting Uncle Frank's life in one way or another. Mindless arguments and pettiness was how he put it. He detested the man but thought a lot of Gillian. To me, Danny was probably jealous of my uncle and the affection he received from his wife."

"Do you think there was something going on between them?"

"No way. Uncle Frank thought of her as a friend, nothing more. He definitely wasn't the type to go after another man's wife. Don't forget there was a good twenty- to twenty-five-year age gap between them as well."

That didn't mean a thing to Sara, she'd heard about people having flings with a partner forty years their junior in her time back in Liverpool. "I see. Do you know if Frank kept any money at the farm?"

"Yes, all of it, I mean, everything he had was kept in a safe in his bedroom. He always told me he didn't trust banks. Called them robbing bastards, especially nowadays with the pitiful interest they're dishing out to savers."

Sara smiled. "Disheartening, I know."

"Why do you ask?"

Choosing to dodge her question for now, Sara asked, "Do you know how much money he had, roughly?"

"No. He was a very private man where his finances were concerned. He never lived beyond his means, only bought the food that was necessary to live on for a few days. His cupboards were virtually bare. Why?" Sadie asked again.

Sara inhaled a large breath then let it out slowly. "Because the safe was open when we checked around his house, and it was empty."

"Oh shit! Are you telling me this was a burglary then? Someone stole his money and killed him into the bargain?"

"So it would seem, yes. Unless we can prove otherwise."

Her eyes narrowed. "I know what I want to suggest but don't want you to think badly of me."

"Go on, we're on a fishing expedition for clues, Sadie, I won't hold anything you tell me against you."

"What if Danny Jenkinson killed my uncle?"

"I find that hard to believe. For one thing, there was a bunch of crime scene investigators at Danny's house when your uncle was killed not to mention a PC in his house at the time of Frank's murder."

"Maybe he paid someone to do it, have you thought about that?"

Sara turned to face Carla who raised an eyebrow. *No, we hadn't thought about that aspect at all.*

"It's definitely something we'll be exploring over the next few days. Is there anything in Frank's past that we should be aware of? Any money problems? Could he have got in with the wrong crowd a few years back, something that might have come back to haunt him, cause him trouble?"

"I can't think of anything. He's lived at the farm for years, didn't really mix with other people, only his family and a few get-togethers with the neighbours at the livestock auctions, that sort of thing. Kept his nose clean, he did. Cared for his animals, and that made his life happy and complete. Oh God, thank goodness he didn't have any pups available. I'll drop by and see if the dogs are all right and get some advice on what to do with them from the rescue centre I know up the road."

"That'll be great, I was concerned about the dogs but forgot to check if there were any in the barn before I left the farm. Okay, well, I suppose we'd better get on our way. We have two cases that need our urgent attention now instead of only the one we began the day with."

Sadie saw them to the front door. "Will you keep me informed?"

Sara nodded. "Of course. The pathologist will be in touch soon, she'll probably need you to make a formal ID. I'm sorry, if that's not what you wanted to hear."

"I'll do it. I'd rather do it than have Mum go through that awful experience, anyway."

"Thanks for speaking with us, I'm so sorry for your loss."

"Thank you, it means a lot."

Sadie closed the front door gently.

Sara and Carla made their way back down the stairs towards the car.

"Interesting what she had to say about Danny. I wasn't surprised by the revelation, though, were you?" Carla asked.

Sara dropped down a couple of steps and replied, "He's definitely someone we need to keep a close eye on, although I stand by what I said back there. In my opinion, I don't think he could have possibly done it, not with all the bodies—sorry poor choice of words—all the tech people outside his place at the time of the other murder. Which leads me to think there's something more going on in the community than we first thought."

"Maybe."

"These cases aren't going to be easy to solve, not with the details we've managed to establish so far. Let's get back to the station. I need an adrenaline-rush-filled coffee to help my brain to function properly."

"I agree. Mine's gone to mush, and we've only just begun."

*B*ack in the incident room, the rest of the team were hard at it and getting nowhere fast.

Sara filled them in on what they'd learned so far. Jill tentatively raised her hand to interrupt.

"We're not in the classroom, Jill, speak freely."

"Something occurred to me earlier, so I did some digging of my own. I hope you don't mind, boss."

"Why should I? I always appreciate members of my team working on their own initiative. What's up?"

"I looked into whether Gillian had a life insurance policy."

"And? Did she?" Sara replied.

Jill nodded. "Yep, for two hundred and fifty grand."

"When was it taken out?"

Jill ran a finger down her notebook. "Back in February, this year."

Sara contemplated this for a second and then snapped her fingers together. "Around the time the notes started appearing. Very interesting indeed."

"What are you thinking?" Carla sipped at her coffee.

"Two scenarios immediately spring to mind. The first that Danny panicked when he received the notes—wait, did he insure himself at the same time, Jill?"

"He did, and the children, which I thought was strange."

"Hmm…it does seem to be odd. Not sure I've heard of anyone insuring their kids before, or is that me simply being clueless about these things?"

"I haven't either," Jill replied. "You were saying, boss?"

The phone rang on Jill's desk, and she answered it.

87

"Ah, yes, either what I said about the first scenario, or Danny is behind all of this. What does everyone else think?"

Jill waved the phone at her and mouthed, 'It's DCI Price wanting a word with you'.

Sara crossed the room and took the phone from Jill. "Hello, ma'am, what can I do for you?"

"In my office at once, DI Ramsey. Don't dilly-dally either."

"On my way." She gave the phone back to Jill and cringed. "I've been summoned. Talk through the different scenarios amongst yourselves, and we'll pick this up when I get back. Wish me luck."

Everyone called out their best wishes as Sara sped out of the room and up the corridor to the Lioness' Den. Her adrenaline pumped her blood around her veins faster than molten lava. It felt just as hot, too.

Mary, DCI Price's PA, was on her feet and holding the door open for her. "Good luck," she whispered. "DI Ramsey to see you, ma'am."

"Thank you, Mary. Get us both a coffee, will you? Take a seat, Inspector."

"Have I done something wrong?"

"You tell me, have you?"

Sara closed her eyes as it dawned on her why her boss had requested her company. "I take it Danny Jenkinson has been in touch with you."

"He has. Now, why should he feel the need to ring me, do you think?"

"It's all quite innocent, if you're prepared to hear me out and not judge me from the outset."

Carol Price wagged her finger. "Cut the crap, stop being so defensive. When have I not stood in your corner?"

"Fair comment. I apologise. In all honesty, I get the impression that Danny doesn't take kindly to women being around him."

"Are you telling me he's a misogynist?"

"That's how it's coming across to me. I think he'd rather have one of my male colleagues working the case than me and Carla."

"What, in your opinion, has given him cause to think that?"

"I haven't got a clue. The more I get to know about him, the more I think it's nothing personal, it's just the way he is."

"And how is the investigation progressing, may I ask?"

"You can ask. Not very well."

The chief opened her mouth to speak, but Sara raised a hand to halt her.

"In our defence, we were called to another crime scene soon after his wife's body was discovered."

"Are you telling me you're leaving his case and moving on to another so soon?"

"Not in the slightest. I believe, as does the pathologist," she added, covering her back, "that both crimes are connected."

"How so? Didn't the wife die when a car exploded? Are you telling me someone else has passed away in the same manner?"

"No, sorry for not explaining myself properly. We were called to a neighbour's farm. Frank Dobbs. Carla and I visited the man a few hours before his demise."

"Goodness me. So there's something far more sinister going on than you first suspected, is that it?"

"So it would seem, yes. The postman called it in. He found Dobbs lying on his drive; he'd been shot twice, we suspect with his own gun, although that is yet to be confirmed. I also noticed that any money he'd been keeping in a safe had been stolen because it was empty when I discovered it in the bedroom."

"Couldn't this be just a coincidence? A burglary gone wrong?"

"Hard to believe, in the circumstances, ma'am."

The door opened, and Mary entered carrying two mugs of coffee.

"Thank you, Mary, close the door on your way out."

"Yes, ma'am."

"Where were we? Ah yes, you were about to tell me why you don't believe this is a burglary gone wrong."

"I can't explain it, ma'am. Other than to say it's far too coincidental for my liking."

"Have you searched the records to see if there were other related crimes in the area?"

"We have. The team couldn't find anything at all. Carla and I just broke the news to Mr Dobbs' niece, and she told us that he had been involved in several arguments with Danny Jenkinson over the past few months. Mr Dobbs himself told us that earlier. Plus, their other neighbour said virtually the same."

"This other neighbour, is he all right?"

"Yes, I have him under guard, if you like. Two PCs are out there at present."

"Good, I was about to suggest the same. What's your thinking on this Danny Jenkinson?"

"I'm in two minds. While I feel sorry for what he's going through, I've spoken to several people during the day, including the reverend of the parish, and none of them have a good word to say about him. Does that excuse what he's going through? No, I don't think it does. I'm going to do my best with the hand I've been dealt. Until we get the results back from the PM, we're still treating his wife's death as an accident, however, the same can't be said for Frank Dobbs. We know that Danny had received some threatening notes in recent months, so maybe I'm doing him a grave injustice. Saying that, I arranged for an FLO to call and see him. Carla and I were at the farm when she showed up. He treated her abysmally, told her to do one. I'm concerned about how he's going to deal with his two kids, which is why I made the arrangements for the FLO to be there with him."

"I see. He seems to be a complex character. He's reported you, that much is evident, right?"

"Yes. I honestly haven't done anything wrong. I did shout at him for the way he treated the FLO, though—after all, we're all doing our best to help the man in his darkest hours."

"I don't know what to suggest. I told him I'd have a word with you and report back to him. I'll tell him that I'm satisfied with how you're conducting the investigation and to give you a chance. I've already told him you're my best copper and I have every faith in your sublime abilities."

Sara chuckled. "Sublime abilities, I like that, maybe I'll use that as my epitaph."

Carol Price smiled for the first time since Sara had entered her office. "That won't happen for years, I hope. Do you need any help on this one?"

"Hard to say at present, ma'am. We've only been on the case since around nine this morning."

The phone interrupted their conversation. "Just a tick, stay there." Carol answered the phone, and her eyes immediately widened. "Okay, calm down, sir. I'll send DI Ramsey out there to see you now... Yes, I've had a word with her. I think you should give her a chance. I assure you, she has your best interests at heart. Hang in there."

"Was that him?" Sara asked as Carol hung up.

"You're never going to believe this...his kids have been abducted."

5

Sara darted out of the chief's office, leaving her half-drunk coffee and a bewildered-looking superior in her wake. *Shit! Shit! Shit!*

She poked her head around the door to the incident room. "Carla, with me. The Jenkinsons' kids have been abducted."

"Fuck," Carla shouted. She tore her jacket off the back of her chair and followed Sara down the stairs at breakneck speed.

"Jeff, I need all available cars out to Northcott Farm."

Startled by her sudden appearance, Jeff clutched at his chest and asked, "May I ask why, ma'am?"

"The two Jenkinson children have been abducted, they're five and six. We need to find them pronto. I want all access roads to that village blocked off. No one goes in or out unless their cars are thoroughly searched, you hear me?" Sara's heart was pounding that hard she could hear it.

"On it right away, ma'am."

She continued out to the car and sucked in lungfuls of fresh air, Carla right behind her, before she slotted behind the steering wheel. "Hang on tight."

Carla secured her seat belt, heeding the warning. "Drive carefully, this isn't worth killing ourselves for."

Sara glanced her way and smiled. "I'm eager to get there, I didn't say I was contemplating a suicide mission, partner."

"Just saying. What do you know about this?"

"Only that Danny rang while I was receiving a bollocking from the chief. She told me to get over there right away. I didn't hang around to ask anything further. Jesus, am I to blame for this?"

"Why think that? You're being absurd. How could we have known something like this would happen on top of everything else today?"

"I don't know, I'm bound to have doubts. What gets to me is that whoever is doing this is having a right laugh at us. Maybe I should've issued the orders to search the area after the first incident happened."

"And have fifty coppers getting in SOCOs' way? No, you've done nothing wrong, despite Jenkinson thinking to the contrary. Put another way, if I were in your shoes and in charge, I definitely wouldn't have done anything different. Christ, we haven't sodding stopped all day, it's not like we went back to the station and sat on our arses doing nothing, is it?"

"I know. I'm being too harsh on myself, there, I've said it." She dodged around a couple of slow-moving cars and sped up the hill past one of their favourite haunts, the Queenswood Café. "What I wouldn't give for one of their calorie-laden cakes right now."

Carla chuckled. "You read my mind. What are we going to do when we get there...? Sorry, that came out wrong. What I meant to say was, what if he's still angry with us? How do we conduct ourselves?"

"The same as we always do, with professionalism. My take is that we're going to see a totally different side of him when we arrive—don't quote me on that, though. Something about vulnerable kids going missing tends to drastically alter a person's outlook."

"No shit! God, I hope we can find them. It's so damn frustrating to think we have no leads yet, two deaths and two abductions in the same day and not a scooby doo what the fuck is going on or who is to blame for these crimes."

"I know, bloody terrible. I hate being in this position. I feel so inept and yet I'm aware at the same time that there is nothing we could have done differently."

"Too right. Did the chief really come down heavy on you?"

"No, not really. I explained the situation to her, and she gave me her full backing, as usual. She accepted it was probably Jenkinson's state of mind and the trauma he was going through."

"That's fair enough. We have a nigh on impossible job on our hands trying to help someone who refuses to acknowledge our help, anyone can see that. Shit, if only he had allowed Annabelle to stay with him, this wouldn't have likely happened, would it?"

"We can't possibly know that until we've heard how the abduction took place or where. Let's not speculate too much for now."

Ten minutes later, they arrived at Northcott Farm. The driveway was clear of SOCO techs, and Jenkinson's vehicle had been removed from the area. It was eerily quiet.

Sara shuddered. "I've got an ominous feeling hanging over me."

"Don't say that." Carla also shuddered.

"Let's go face the music." Sara got out of the car and cocked her head. In the distance were sirens drawing closer. "Wait, before we go ahead and knock on his door, I think I should direct the attending officers on what to do."

Carla scratched her head. "With respect, how can you do that without speaking to him first? He needs to tell us accurately what went down before you can issue any orders, right?"

Sara winked at her. "I was testing you, just to see if you still had your eye on the ball."

"Yeah, right. I believe you."

"I'll see what he has to say, you deal with the team when they arrive. I should have some news for you soon."

"Good luck, I have a feeling you're going to need it."

"Cheers." Sara rushed across the drive and knocked on the front door.

It was swiftly opened by a dishevelled-looking Danny. He had blood streaming down his face from a head wound.

"Shit. Are you all right?"

He staggered backwards. "I'll be all right. I want my children back. You have to find them."

"We'll do that, I promise you. First, you're going to have to tell me what happened."

He walked into the kitchen. Sara shut the front door and followed him.

He sank into a chair at the table and placed a hand on either side of his head as if to support it. "Why? Why is this happening to me? Haven't I suffered enough today already? Why is someone punishing me like this? I want my children back before he kil—"

"You mustn't think like that. I have a whole squad of uniformed police on the way. If they're out there, we'll find them, you have my word. Please, take a breath and tell me what happened."

"I saw the SOCO guys off the premises around threeish and then wandered down to the school to collect the children rather than wait for the bus to arrive. I needed the exercise and thought the fresh air would do me some good. I collected the children, spoke to some of the women also doing the school run. They commiserated with me over Gillian's passing. Everything was fine, the kids were skipping along, enjoying themselves, blissfully unaware of what had gone on with their mother. I had no intention of telling them so soon."

"You walked all the way back home? Following the road, or did you cut across the fields?"

"If you'll let me finish," he snapped.

"Sorry, please continue." She leaned against the doorframe and folded her arms.

Danny's gaze dropped back to the cruet set in the centre of the table. "We were chatting away, or the kids were. Always chattering on about something or other, those two. I didn't hear anyone approach. Tammy stopped talking and turned to speak to someone. That's when I got whacked around the head. I fell to the ground immediately. The kids' screams will live with me forever." His teary eyes met hers. "Please, you have to help me find them. I don't know what all this is about. Why someone would intentionally go after my family like this, but I need it to stop. I want my kids back. I didn't know it was going to go this far...the notes...I took them to the station and was ignored. Now look what I'm dealing with, my wife's dead and my two young kids are missing. Lord knows what the hell is going to happen to them. Oh God, I can't think about that. Please, you have to get them back. Without them I'm nothing."

"Please, you need to remain positive. We're going to do our best to bring them home to you. Can you think of anyone who would want to do these dreadful things to you and your family?"

"No, I've sat here all day, trying my hardest to search for a name to give you, apart from those I've already told you about, of course."

"Your two neighbours?"

"Yes, they've both had it in for me for a while. All right, Dobbs is out of the picture now, but what about the other one? You need to get over there and question him. He's the only one who comes to mind who could possibly hate me so much."

"I'll visit him again, but I have to tell you we've had two uniformed officers outside his property since lunchtime. So I think it would be highly unlikely to be Andy."

His head rose, and he glared at her. "You what? Why are you giving him preferential treatment? Why?"

"We're not, not really. I made the call to protect him after the incident with your wife this morning, and, well, Frank's murder this afternoon, plus you asked the PC and the FLO to leave. My instinct told me that Andy could be the next target."

"That's bullshit. This is about me and my family. He did this, I'm telling you, whether he was under armed guard or not."

"Not armed, I never said that. Let me shoot over there, if that would put your mind at ease. Will you be okay until I get back? You should have someone look at your injury."

He waved his hand. "I'm fine. Yes, go and see the bastard, torture him if you need to, I demand to know what he's done with my children. I want them back! I'll not rest until they're here with me again."

"Don't worry, we're on the case. We'll find them sooner or later."

"Search his house!"

"I'll do that, although I think it will be a waste of my time, he's been under observation. Let me go over there now, I'll speak to you when I get back."

"You do that. Don't take any obvious shit from him. If Dobbs wasn't behind the notes and everything that's gone on since, then he's the one. You should take him down the station, use FBI torture tactics if necessary. My kids are in danger for fuck's sake, and you're stood here arguing the toss with me whether he could be responsible or not."

"I think you're being unreasonable, and just to clarify something, the police don't torture people here in the UK. We have a set protocol in place. Whether that person is a two-bit chancer of a burglar or a violent serial killer."

"Whatever. You're wasting time telling me all this shit, my kids' lives are in mortal danger. You need to recognise that when you're speaking to the fucker, got that?"

"Loud and clear. I'll be back soon." Sara dashed out of the house and approached Carla who was issuing orders to the uniformed men gathered around her. She stopped talking when Sara joined her. "Guys, I want everywhere searched. I know we haven't got much light left, but those kids are in danger. It's imperative we find them. We've set up roadblocks. The father picked the kids up from school, he was on foot, someone whacked him over the head and took the kids between here and the primary school in the village. Yes, we could be too late. My take is that's probably the case, given the time that's elapsed. If someone had the intention of kidnapping two kids, they must have had an escape plan in place. Let's disregard that for now and just concentrate our efforts on searching the vicinity just in case the kidnapper didn't have a plan in place and panicked once the kids started screaming or something." Sara clapped to dismiss the officers.

Carla flicked her head at the farmhouse. "How is he?"

"Much as you would expect, distraught about his kids and adamant that Andy is the culprit. I've explained the situation about Andy being under guard today. He seemed shocked to hear that at first which gave way to infuriation. To calm him down I told him I would pay Andy a visit. So we'll go over there now."

"What? And leave him here alone? What if the killer comes back?"

"Okay, there is that. Hi, you two stragglers, stay here until we get back. Mr Jenkinson is inside the house. Make sure he stays here. I have a feeling he might try to follow us. We'll be fifteen minutes tops, okay?"

The male officer nodded. "We'll stay outside, ma'am."

Sara motioned for Carla to get in the car and sped off, the gravel scattering in all the directions of a compass in her wake. "I think he's talking bullshit, trying to apportion the blame, but I think he's wrong."

"What else can he do? He sounds desperate. He's not likely to do anything, you know, to himself, is he?"

Sara sighed and cringed. "If we don't get the kids back then I dread to think what he'll be capable of. We have to get them back, Carla, we just have to."

"Poor buggers. Who would put little mites like them through shit like this, after losing their mum today as well?"

"God knows, because I'm struggling to get a handle on it."

Another few hundred yards, and Sara drew into Andy's drive. The two uniformed officers standing at the front door acknowledged her and Carla as they walked up to the farmhouse.

Sara lowered her voice to ask, "Has he left the house at all?"

"No, ma'am. He's popped out several times to supply us with a drink, but apart from that, no, we haven't seen him. Is something wrong?"

"Yes, very wrong. Okay, I'm going in."

The two officers glanced at each other and shrugged.

Sara eased open the front door. "Andy, it's DI Ramsey, is it all right if I come in?"

Andy appeared in the hallway and beckoned her. "Of course, do you have news for me?"

"Sort of."

They went into the lounge. Carla joined them after she'd closed the front door.

Andy appeared fraught with tension and ran a shaking hand around his face. "What news do you have? I've been on tenterhooks all afternoon, since your last visit."

"We have some news for you. It's not great. I think you'd better sit down."

He slumped onto the sofa and waited until Sara and Carla had sat, then asked, "Not another murder? Is Danny all right? They haven't got to him, have they? Or anyone else? Jesus, all this is making me a bloody nervous wreck. I'm sorry, I'll keep quiet."

Sara smiled, trying to put the man at ease. "We've just come from Northcott Farm. Danny called the station this afternoon to tell us that his children, Tammy and Ben, have been abducted."

"What? Bloody hell, this day is getting worse by the damn second. Why? Do you know who has taken them? Lordy, they'll be petrified. All this on top of losing their beautiful mother. What in God's name is going on?"

Sara tutted. "We're no nearer to finding out who the culprit is. Our investigation hasn't had a chance to take off yet, what with all that's gone on."

"Do you think that's the bastard's intention? To keep you on your toes?"

"Maybe, it does seem that way."

"Is he all right? Danny?"

"He's nursing a wounded head where the perpetrator whacked him before they took the kids."

"Were there any witnesses? Where did this happen?"

"No witnesses, not that we know of anyway. He'd picked them up from school and was walking home with them."

He placed a hand over his eyes, and his shoulders jiggled. "Not the kids, please, don't let anything bad happen to them, they don't deserve any of this."

Andy appeared to be traumatised by the news. "We'll get them back."

He dropped his hand and shook his head. "None of what has gone on today is making any sense to me. If someone has a vendetta against

Danny, why punish his family like this? Why not have it out with him and be done with it?"

"Precisely. We're at a loss where to turn. He's pointed the finger at you and Frank. I didn't mean it like that, all I meant was when I asked him who he'd fallen out with recently he said you and Frank and no one else."

"Neither one of us would dream of hurting the family, they were minor squabbles in my mind. I could never contemplate hurting another human being, no matter how much I detested that person. I don't have it in me to harm someone, you have to believe me."

"I do. I'm not saying you're involved at all. But there's no doubting that someone is. A complete stranger that has it in for the family."

"I can understand that, but why kill Frank as well? What's he got to do with anything?" Andy asked, his eyes narrowing as he thought.

"Again, at the moment, that's a mystery to us. We're going to canvass the whole community, starting tomorrow. Someone must know something, must have seen a perfect stranger hanging around."

"You're presuming this is all down to an outsider. What if it isn't?"

"Again, only interviewing the community will give us a possible answer. For now, our main priority has to be the children and returning them to their grieving father."

"I agree. Can I offer a hand in trying to find them? Let's face it, I know the area better than you guys."

"That's kind of you to offer, but I'd still like to keep you safe, under observation for the next day or two, if you don't mind?"

"Sure. However, I have to say that's going to be frustrating for me, knowing those two cherished children are out there, or should I say, in the hands of a stranger." He closed his eyes and shook his head. "Lord knows what will happen to them."

"It's best not to consider the consequences, years of experience has told me that much, Andy. Okay, we're going to get back to Danny now. I wanted to come over here to fill you in and check everything was all right."

"I'm fine. Send him my best wishes, tell him I'll be praying the kids are safely returned, unharmed."

"I'll pass on that message. Stay vigilant at all times, promise me."

"I will. I have company outside my front door. I feel sorry for them, can't they come inside, in the warm?"

"Yes, that's acceptable. I'll invite them in on my way out. Try not to worry too much."

"Easier said than done, I fear, Inspector. Can I feed the officers? Is that permitted?"

"I don't see why not. You're not obliged to, though, Andy."

"I know. Just trying to show my appreciation. I hope you find the little darlings soon and I also hope that Gillian is watching over them, keeping them safe."

"So do I. We'll be in touch if we hear anything further."

He showed them to the door.

"Guys, Andy's kindly offered to cook you a meal. You're welcome to come inside for the rest of your shift on one proviso, you remain vigilant at all times, got that?"

Both PCs smiled and nodded. "That's great. Thank you, sir, ma'am."

"Come on in. How does a good fry-up sound, lads?" Andy gestured for the men to enter the house and waved at Sara and Carla before the door closed.

Once they were back in the car, Sara asked her partner to call the station and request that four members of the team join them. "We should get them to start canvassing all the houses in the main village, the ones near the school and along the route Danny took home, see if anyone saw anything. We can't be seen to be doing nothing otherwise Danny will put in another complaint against me."

"I'll do it now. I agree, it's the way to go."

Sara drove back to Danny's and parked the car close to the farm-house once more.

Carla ended the call as she drew up. "All sorted. Christine and Jill are going to remain behind. Will, Barry, Craig and Marissa are heading out to join us."

"Fantastic. I'll just ring Mark, let him know that I'll be late home. I'll be with you in a tick."

Carla took the intended hint and exited the car.

Sara rang her husband's mobile.

He answered instantly. "Wow, how did you know?"

"How did I know what?" She glanced around at the several barns lining the courtyard, an idea forming in her mind.

"That I was about to call you."

"You were? Anything wrong?"

"Umm…I wanted to warn you that I could be late home this evening. I have an emergency on the way in. A boxer got run over, he has a shattered leg I need to repair. Depending how bad it is, I could be in surgery for anything up to five or six hours. I won't know for certain until I take an x-ray when the owner brings him in."

"Oh, how dreadful, that poor dog. I hope it's not as bad as you think it is. And snap, I was calling you to say the same thing. That I'm going to be late, not that I have a boxer in need of assistance." She chuckled. It felt good to ease the tension tightening the muscles in her shoulders.

"Damn. Why? And that'll teach us both having time off to get married and enjoy a honeymoon, won't it?"

"You're not wrong, I was thinking the same thing a few hours ago. Possible double murder, plus I've just been notified that two children have been abducted. Every available copper is out here, searching for the little ones."

"Crap, and it'll be getting dark soon. You have my sympathy. You and your team haven't got the easiest of tasks ahead of you."

"No kidding. I haven't got a clue what time I'll be home, depends if we find them or not. If we don't, then I think I'll probably work through."

"I hope you find them for your sake. Have you eaten?"

Her stomach grumbled at the question. "I had a sandwich earlier on. We'll ring for pizza if we have time later. Don't fret about me. I'll be fine."

"I know what you're like, you've been known to forget to eat once you're knee-deep in a case. Don't do it, Sara, promise me?"

"I promise. I've got to dash. Hope the op goes well."

"Thanks. Give me a call later, let me know how you're getting on. Sending positive thoughts out to keep those kiddies safe. I love you, Sara Ramsey-Fisher."

"Oo...I like the idea of having a double-barrelled name. One to consider for sure. I love you, too."

His laugh trickled down the line as she hit the End Call button. She left the vehicle and strolled across the courtyard to the first barn.

Carla joined her and said, "What are you thinking? The kids could be in here?"

"That hadn't really crossed my mind, but now you've mentioned it, shit, we're in a farming community, can you imagine the number of outbuildings there must be in this area where the perp could be hiding the kids?"

Carla tutted. "It doesn't bear thinking about. That's if the bastard is still around. My guess is that he probably left the area swiftly, just in case it was locked down once the word got out. Did Danny lose consciousness?"

"I believe so, although he never really said, I suppose I just presumed he had, taking into consideration the whack he'd taken."

"Are we ever likely to find them?"

Sara faced Carla and tilted her head. "What sort of question is that? It's not like you to give up on someone so soon, matey."

"I'm not. I suppose I'm just voicing what dozens of other officers have running through their mind at the moment. Kids are perceived as a valuable commodity to some, you know that as well as I do."

"Jesus, don't you think I'm aware of that fact? I've pushed that thought aside for now and I'd rather you did the same. How is thinking along those lines going to help solve this case, Carla?"

Her head dipped, and she mumbled an apology. "Sorry, maybe it was wrong of me to voice my opinion."

"No, it wasn't. We have to be mindful of both sides, I appreciate that. Hey, don't feel bad, although I'm glad you aired your thoughts only to me."

"Yeah, I'd never have said the same thing if we were in a team meeting, I promise."

"Good. It's forgotten. I just want to have a quick nose around in here before we go back in the house to see Danny."

"Makes sense."

They rooted around the first barn which was full of essential food for the livestock, nothing out of the ordinary coming to light there. Then they moved on to the second barn which was full of farming equipment, both large and small. Lots of nooks and crannies where a child might be hidden, but after a thorough search of the interior, they left feeling disappointed.

"Come on, let's go back inside and see how Danny is. We'll get uniform to continue the search out here later."

"You really think it's worthwhile? I mean, wouldn't their resources be needed elsewhere? How likely is it the perp would use Danny's barns to imprison his own kids?"

"Okay, you've got me on that one, it'll be a waste of time. I'm tired and guess I'm guilty of not thinking straight."

They entered the front door of the farmhouse and caught Danny just going up the stairs. He stumbled, lost his balance and ended up bashing against the wall.

Sara leapt to his assistance. "Oh gosh, are you all right?"

"It's my damn head. It's doing a number on me. One minute I'm fine, the next I'm dizzy and flolloping all over the place." He unhitched his arm from hers.

"Where are you going? You should be resting, better still, you should be in hospital, Danny. It's possible you've got concussion."

"I refuse to go to hospital. I need to be here in case you find my kids." His gaze bored into hers. "You will find them, won't you? They don't deserve any of this. They're good kids. They'll be terrified without their mum or me being with them."

"Try not to upset yourself. We have the biggest manhunt underway that this county has ever experienced. What you need to do is take care of yourself, to stay fit and well for when they return. They're going to need their dad to be on the ball."

"If you put it that way, yes, I suppose you have a point. Would you mind helping me upstairs? I don't have a downstairs loo and I'm busting to go for a wee."

"Too much information there, Danny." She smiled and hooked an arm through his. "Come on, let's get you up there before we have a puddle to clear up."

Sara deposited him in the bathroom at the top of the stairs and closed the door. "Leave it unlocked, I promise not to peek."

She heard him having a widdle, and the chain flushed not long after. He washed his hands in the sink, then there was silence as he presumably dried them. The door opened, and he staggered out.

"How are you feeling now?"

"Relieved." He smiled tautly and winced. "My head is throbbing rhythmically to Jamaican drums, at least that's what it seems like. Will it get better?"

"In time. Look, while we're up here, why don't you have a lie-down? We'll keep an eye on proceedings downstairs, while you have a quick nap. I'm sure you'll feel a whole lot better and able to cope afterwards."

He chewed on his bottom lip. "Okay, I think you're right. Can you help me to my room, it's at the end of the passage?"

They linked arms again, and Sara took the strain as he leaned on her for support.

"Is this it?"

"Yes." He hesitated in the doorway, his feet appearing to be ton weights all of a sudden.

"Are you all right?"

He shook his head and winced again. "No, I can't go in there. It's full of her things. It'll be too much too soon. Maybe I'll take a nap in the kids' room, yes, that's what I'll do. At least I'll feel like I'm near them in one sense."

Sara could tell he was about to break down the second he stepped into the kids' room. She prepared herself and backed up at the doorway to give him space to come to terms with his loss all over again. "I'm so sorry. Please, try not to upset yourself. Maybe it would be better to sleep in a spare room if you have one."

"We haven't. Not one that's set up as a bedroom anyway. I'll be fine once I get my head around it. I need to be close to them, to their things."

He gingerly entered the room and walked over to the bed underneath the window on the right. It was a dual aspect bedroom, with two beds and a single wardrobe in the corner and a chest of drawers sitting under the other window. He settled onto the bed, snatched up the brown teddy lying on the pillow and nestled his head in its place. "I think I'll just have forty winks, if you don't mind?"

The caring side of Sara wanted to pick his feet up and place them on the bed, but something prevented her from doing it. "Can I get you a blanket?"

He scooped a hand behind him and tugged at the length of quilt draping down the side of the bed and pulled it over him. "This will do. Thanks. Find my kids, please."

Sara smiled down at him; he was on the verge of drifting off already. "We will. Sleep well."

"Goodnight," he whispered. His voice was replaced almost instantly by the sound of heavy breathing and then a snore.

She crept out of the room and closed the door to behind her, leaving it slightly ajar.

Entering the lounge, she let out a huge sigh. "That's him sorted for a few hours. Fancy a coffee?"

"Why not? Maybe we can do some brainstorming with him out of the way. One question."

"Go on." Sara paused at the door to the kitchen.

"Why hasn't he cleaned his head up? The blood, it would be the first thing you or I would have done in the same circumstances, wouldn't it?"

"Maybe he had and it's continued to bleed, have you thought about that?"

Carla cringed. "Nope. Sorry. Ignore me."

"Christ, the number of times you've muttered those words lately, it's a wonder we manage to solve any case with your input."

Carla gasped. "Charming."

"I was joking. Coffee coming up. I wonder if we can have a sneaky biscuit or two in his absence."

"At your own risk, I'd say. He seems the type to count what's in the bloody biscuit barrel."

"You reckon? I'll give that a miss then. The drink should fill a hole for now."

Sara entered the kitchen and resisted the temptation to have a nose in what she perceived to be a pantry over in the right-hand corner. There was a latch on the door which she presumed would be noisy to open and might possibly alert Danny in the room overhead of her intentions.

Instead, she boiled the kettle and made two coffees.

Carla was peering out of the window in the lounge upon her return. "All quiet out there."

"Everyone has been given their tasks. Fingers crossed someone comes up trumps tonight, it's been a hell of a day so far. I don't relish it being an all-nighter. Take a seat, we'll discuss things quietly over our drink. Push the door to on your way, will you?"

Carla did just that and parked her backside close to Sara on the large comfy couch. "Maybe we should sit at the kitchen table, in case we get too comfortable and drift off."

"No fear of that happening, my brain is in overdrive. No chance of it shutting down anytime soon. Let's try and work out any connections we might have missed in the case so far."

Carla pulled a face. "Such as? Bloody hell, to my mind we've got virtually nothing to go on. What have we got, seriously? A family car which exploded while their other car is being serviced at the garage because its brake lines have been cut. Then we got called to Frank Dobbs' gaff to find he'd been shot twice with his own rifle. Before he carked it—sorry to be so blunt—before he passed away, he couldn't tell us anything other than he'd had several arguments with Danny..." Carla pointed at the ceiling. "Not only that, the other neighbour, Andy Brady, told us virtually the same. Both men can't be wrong, can they? Then we get a call to come back here and find Danny's children have been abducted. Again, no clues as to who the fuck has it in for this bloke, his family and his neighbour. Did I miss anything out?"

Sara bit her lip and shook her head. "I don't think so. We can't keep saying we haven't got a clue, it won't wash with DCI Price for a start, let alone the Super, hon."

"I know, but we can't falsify evidence or make it up just to suit our needs, can we?"

"I wouldn't want to go down that route. I've never gone to those lengths in the past, I'm not about to start now, no matter how frustrating all this might be."

"So, what's the answer?"

"We sit here in the hope that the team and uniform uncover something useful. Which leads me to another point."

"Which is?"

"I hate the thought of sitting on my hands and babysitting someone who has just issued a bloody complaint against me."

"I can see how upsetting that could be for you. Broad shoulders and all that."

"Yeah, let it wash off, it still sticks in the throat, though."

They went back and forth with possible scenarios as to what was behind all that had gone on during the day until an hour or so later. A cry from upstairs alerted Sara. She'd been drifting off to sleep but was now thundering up the stairs, taking them two at a time. She barged into the kids' bedroom to find Danny huddled up against the headboard, rocking back and forth, the edge of the quilt clutched in his tightly formed hands.

"Danny, are you all right?"

"No, he was here. Haunting my dreams."

Sara moved closer to the bed. "There's no one here, love. It was only a bad dream."

His head shook. "It was so real. Tammy and Ben were crying out for me, shouting that I had let them down and desperate for me to help them. How can I do that when I don't know where they are?"

"You can't. Don't feel bad, all this is out of your control. I'm sure the kids are safe, somewhere close by, waiting for us to find them."

"How can you be certain of that? The truth is, you don't know who is behind all this shit, so how can you possibly know everything is going to be all right and go back to normal soon? None of us know that. Nothing is ever going to be the same again, not with Gillian and the kids gone. Life is no longer worth living. I might as well slit my throat and be done with it. At least it'll deaden the pain."

She inched closer and tried her best to reassure him. "You can't give up, not now, not when they need you the most, Danny. You have to have complete faith and trust in our abilities. I know we got off on the wrong foot, but please, I assure you, I only have your family's best interests at heart."

"Do you? Why are you here then and not out there getting involved in the search?"

"Because I thought it would be best to remain here with you, given your injury."

"Why? You think this madman is going to come back and finish off the job, don't you? To kill me?"

"No, that's not what I think at all. Don't say that. I truly believe he won't come back, not while there's a huge police presence in the village."

"Can you guarantee that? Because the bastard has already come back to kill Frank and to kidnap my kids, and you did little to prevent him from doing that, from what I can remember."

Sara shrugged. What could she say in response to him pointing out the truth? "That was different."

"How? The SOCO people were still around in force when Frank got killed, and they'd not long left the property when Tammy and Ben were taken. I think you're guilty of not taking this person seriously. It's obvious he has an agenda and is not bothered who he kills on the way to achieving his aim." He gasped and slapped a hand over his mouth. Tears tumbled onto his flushed cheeks. He dropped his hand into his lap and whispered, "What am I saying? He's going to kill them, isn't he? It has to be running through his mind, as much as it's going through mine. Bloody hell, I've failed to protect them, and now they're at his mercy. Shit! What have I done?"

Sara sat close to him on the bed and placed a hand over his. "You've done nothing wrong. Stop punishing yourself like that, you have to, otherwise you'll end up going insane, Danny. I repeat, give us a chance to get you reunited with your kids. I'm sorry you're going through this torment and trauma, especially after losing Gillian this morning, but please, whatever you do, don't give up on your kids, or us, not yet."

"Words are cheap, Inspector. It's actions I need. My desire to have my kids back is all I have to cling on to. You need to leave me and join the search. Do something out there, instead of sitting on your arse here, with me."

"Okay, if that's what you want. Let me call upon someone in the village to come and sit with you then, how's that?"

"No!" he shouted. "Sorry, no, the last thing I want is a bunch of nosey parkers snooping around here, searching for snippets of information to set their gossiping tongues wagging. I want nothing to do with anyone. All I want is my kids back. I need them here with me. I'm nothing otherwise. What the fuck do I have to live for? My livestock? To keep them fed and watered? They're capable of fending for themselves if it comes to the crunch. My kids need their father, now that their mother is no longer walking this earth. We're all we've got. The three of us."

Sara stood and glanced down at him, her heart laying heavily against her stomach. "Please, I know I keep repeating myself, but I'm begging you not to give up on us. It's only been a few hours since they were taken. We have feet on the ground out there doing their very best to find them."

"In the village and the surrounding fields, right?"

"Of course."

He grunted. "That's ludicrous, as if they'd still be around here. Get the helicopters out there searching for my babies. You have to do everything you can to bring them home to me."

"There's one on the way, it's been delayed," she said—it was only a white lie. The crew were on another mission when she'd placed the call. "DS Jameson and I will leave you in peace, if you're sure you'll be okay?"

"Go."

"I'll be in touch the instant we hear anything."

He turned his back on her. Disheartened, she left the house, collecting her partner on the way.

6

_D_espite the helicopter finally showing up to assist with the search, nothing was found. At five minutes past midnight, Sara put an end to the search for the night. It was pointless continuing; everyone's torch batteries were running out by then anyway.

The uniformed officers drifted away, leaving only the members of her team in the centre of the village.

"We've done our best, guys. I had intended working through the night, but to be honest with you, I don't really see the point. Let's go home, get some rest and start all over again tomorrow. What am I saying? It's tomorrow already, you know what I mean. I'll ring the station, let Jill and Christine know the score. I know this has been a frustrating evening for us all, but we need to shrug it off and start anew in the morning. We'll exchange notes, then Carla and I will come back out, speak to the people at the school and see if they either heard or saw something—we arrived too late this afternoon to question anyone there. Go home. Thanks for your concerted efforts today. Carla, jump in, I'll drop you back to the station."

"No, you won't, I'll get a lift with Will. You're not far from home, boss, it would be silly for you to drive all the way into town and back out here again just to drop me off."

Sara smiled and rubbed Carla's arm. "I wasn't thinking straight. Okay, see you in the morning."

She waved the rest of the team off and drove home. She switched off the headlights the second she drew into the road, always considerate of her neighbours. The house was quiet. Her tummy protested that it was running on empty. She closed the door to the kitchen while she prepared a ham and cheese sandwich. She would have preferred something hot like a jacket potato, but time was against her, and her eyelids were already drooping.

The kettle's steam drifted past her face. Sandwich now made, she filled a mug with water, added a spoonful of coffee, sugar and milk and sat at the table. She slipped into autopilot to eat and drink, her mind racing still, trying to figure out where the two children could be. She shook away her darkest thoughts. Now was not the time to consider them, she needed to remain positive that there would be a successful and happy outcome to this traumatic day.

Boy! Has it been tough or what? One suspected murder, another definite murder and on top of that, two kids being abducted literally from under our noses, well, sort of. Who? Why? Does someone truly hate Danny that much? What on earth could he have done that has wronged someone enough to consider doing something as drastic as kidnapping Danny's kids as punishment? No ransom demand has been issued, so this can't be about money, can it? Then there was the money stolen from Frank Dobbs' place.

That's as far as her thoughts went, because let's face it, that's all they damn well had. She completed her supper, it had been a long time since she'd had one of those, switched off the lights and crept up the stairs to bed.

Misty was keeping Mark company, curled up at the end of the bed. Her sudden bout of purring and Mark's gentle snoring were comforting to her. A touch of normality to end her day. She quickly undressed and climbed into bed beside Mark. He stirred and automatically reached out an arm, drawing her into a much-needed cuddle. She kissed him on the nose and whispered, "I love you more than you know, Mr Fisher."

"I know just how much that is, Mrs Fisher," he mumbled.

They kissed and drifted off to sleep, huddled together. Them against the rest of the world.

7

$\mathcal{T}$he man slipped on the clown mask and entered the dark, damp room. The two children were wrapped in each other's arms, the girl whimpering, the little boy telling her to be quiet.

"Shut her up," the man barked out the order in a gruff voice.

The girl's whimpering ceased for a moment but then started up again, only this time it was louder.

The man took a step towards the petrified kids and leaned in to the girl, his nose almost touching hers with just the thick latex in between. "I said, shut up. You want me to return and kill your father? I've already killed your mother. May God take her soul and show mercy on her. She went up in a second. Sadly, her life would have ended quickly. I can rectify that, by going back and torturing your father before I slit his throat. Is that what you want, little girl?"

"No, please…I not want my daddy hurt."

The masked man turned his attention on the brat sitting beside her. "Make sure she keeps her mouth shut. Or I'll kill your father in front of you and then turn my knife on both of you, got that?"

"I'm sorry, yes. Please, she's scared, we both are. She's only five, mister. We want our father, please, don't hurt him."

"Then keep the noise to a minimum. I've brought you some food. Crisps and chocolate, that's what kids love to eat, isn't it?"

"For treats, yes. We eat normal food, too. Do you have fruit, an apple or orange? Tammy loves those little oranges, I don't know what they're called. We always get one in our stocking at Christmas."

"Shut up. Stop wittering on. You have what you're given. You don't get a choice, not around here. Maybe at the end, maybe it'll be different then."

"What…what do you mean?"

He'd said too much, he knew that. The kids were petrified enough already without him hinting at what lay ahead of them. "Eat it."

He backed up a few paces and folded his arms. Stared at them until they nibbled on the food he'd supplied.

The children sipped at the small carton of orange juice which accompanied their unhealthy snack. He remained there with them until they'd eaten. Both kids had good appetites, considering the trauma they were going through.

"Can we go now?" the boy asked, his voice quaking.

"No. You need to stay here a few days. I'll come and feed you regularly, but only if you behave yourselves. One word out of you, and remember, your father will be killed. Got that?"

The boy nodded, and the girl sobbed.

"Got it. We'll be good. I promise we'll be good," Ben said.

"Right. I have to go now. I'm going to switch off the light. There are a few blankets in the carrier bags over there. Make sure you wrap up and keep your sister warm."

"I'll take care of her and…thank you for the food and the blankets."

"Nice to see your parents instilled some manners in you. Be good, stay quiet. One scream and…" He took a knife from his jacket and placed it to his neck. "Your father will get it."

The children nodded, the girl sniffling in between the heart-wrenching sobs. Even the little boy's eyes bulged with tears now.

He turned his back and switched off the light. Two gasps, whispers and sniffles accompanied his journey to the door. A smile stretched his lips apart. He was pleased with how today had panned out. He removed the mask and tucked it into his jacket pocket, ready to use the next day.

8

*S*ara showered early the following morning. Mark made her a couple of pieces of toast and honey to set her up for the day ahead. It was all she wanted after having a late supper only a few hours earlier. She tried to overlook the fact that all her meals the previous day had been loaded with carbs. Maybe cereals would have been a better option this morning.

"How did it go yesterday?" Mark poured the coffee and set her mug down next to the toast on the table.

Sara sat in the chair and nibbled on her breakfast. "It's a tough one. I feel so inadequate, I think we all do. It's going to be about limiting that feeling first thing during the morning meeting. We all worked exceptionally hard yesterday without having anything to show for it."

"Surely you have someone in mind?"

"I wish. The father blamed his neighbours to start with. One of those ended up dead as well."

"That still leaves the other one."

"I don't think it's Andy, he's too nice. Anyway, from lunchtime yesterday I had two PCs standing outside his door, guarding the place in case the killer decided to show up there and bump him off. There's no way he's involved, I'd bet my life on that."

"Where does that leave you then?"

"High and dry with few clues at our disposal to sift through. Frustrating isn't the word, I tell you. It's hard to try and think outside the damn box when you have two kids' lives on your conscience."

He leaned over and kissed her. "Don't do it, love. Don't beat yourself up. You're doing your very best."

She sighed and twisted her mug on the coaster. "It's clearly not good enough, though, Mark."

"You're tired, doubts are bound to seep in. You need to keep them tethered before they fester, love. I have every faith in your abilities."

She smiled and linked fingers with him. "Thank you, that means a lot and will help to set me up for the day, knowing that I have your support."

"Always, never doubt that, Sara. We're a team, right?"

"How was your day?"

His mouth turned down at the sides. "Not the best. I had to amputate the boxer's leg in the end, it was smashed into dozens of pieces. I doubt even Noel Fitzpatrick could have worked his magic on that one." He was referring to the wonderful Supervet and miracle worker of the decade.

"That's a shame. I know you always regard losing a limb as a last resort."

"Never mind. He'll be running around on three legs soon enough. He's got a wonderful spirit."

"I wish we had a dog." She held her hands up, blocking his objection. "I know it's not practical, both of us working full time."

"Maybe we can discuss it in the near future. I could take the dog to work with me, that's always an option."

"Wow, I never thought about that. I'd love one. There are plenty of rescue pups out there, crying out to be loved."

He tipped his head back and laughed. "Umm…yes, I realise that, you know, what with me being a qualified vet."

"Sorry, I wasn't thinking."

"I'll let you off, this time. Right, I've gotta fly. I have a C-section to perform this morning and I need to have a thorough clean down before the patient arrives. I'll see you later. Give me a ring during the day if you get the chance. I'll spend the day with my fingers crossed, in the hope you find those poor kids." He stood and bent to kiss her.

"Leave the dishes, I'll do them before I go. Hope all goes well with the puppies. What is it?"

"A Springer spaniel, a local working dog. She's too young to be having pups in my honest opinion, hence my suggestion to do a C-section. The less stress she has the better, she's flighty at the best of times."

"Ugh…why do owners put their dogs' lives at risk like that?"

"Don't get me started. See you tonight."

He raced out the back door, and then she was left with just Misty as her companion to finish off her breakfast and contemplate what lay ahead of her.

"So, that's where we are, guys. Let's get back out there, knock on every door possible—even if you knocked on it yesterday, do it again. People have had a few hours to reflect now, and hopefully, one of those you've already questioned will come up with an answer or two for us today."

"What about the media?" Carla asked.

"I rang the press officer on my way in this morning, Jane told me to leave it with her. She's going to try and organise a conference for later on this afternoon. With any luck, we'll have a few snippets of information we can give to the public by then. Let's do our best on that front. Jill and Christine, are you two all right manning the phones here?"

"Yes, boss. Give us a shout if you need anything," Jill replied, speaking for both of them.

"We'll keep you updated on our progress. I'm going to call at Northcott Farm first, check in on Danny, see if there's been any change at his end. Okay, gang, let's get going, time being of the essence and all that business."

The team gathered their jackets and set off. Sara and Carla were just about to do the same when DCI Price appeared in the doorway.

"How are things?"

Sara held out a wavering hand. "So-so. We're heading out there again now. We all worked past midnight, until our torches ran out. No sign of the kids at all."

"Have you considered asking the public for help?"

"Yes, Jane is organising a conference for this afternoon. In the meantime, Carla and I will get back out there and start questioning people in the village, at the school et cetera."

"Good. Do you need me to pave the way with anything?"

"I don't think so, boss."

"What about Mr Jenkinson? How's he holding up?"

"We stayed with him while he grabbed a bit of sleep yesterday evening. He took a nasty bang to his head but refused to leave the farmhouse and go to hospital just in case the kids came back in his absence."

"That's understandable. How was he towards you, after issuing his complaint?"

"He seemed okay. I assured him I was the right person to see this case to its conclusion—he accepted that. Of course, his outlook might have changed overnight. We won't know that until we get there and see for ourselves. Talking of which, we'd better shift our backsides, ma'am."

Carol stepped aside. "The last thing I want to do is hold you up. Keep in touch, especially if you find the kiddies. I've barely slept myself last night, worrying about the little buggers. Most unlike me, I usually sleep like a baby."

"It's horrible when a case plays on your mind like that. I think I was too exhausted by the time I got home preventing my brain from kicking in. If you get what I mean?"

"I do. Go. Good luck."

Sara and Carla left the station and drove out to the farm again. There was a light on upstairs and in the lounge. Sara rang the bell. Danny thundered down the stairs to answer it.

"Good morning," Sara said, offering him a warm smile.

"Is it? Have you found them yet?"

"No. We're just about to start again."

He glanced at his watch. "Nice to see you take your job seriously, Inspector."

His barbed retort was to be expected. "We worked until gone midnight, Danny."

"Sorry, I'm aware of that."

"How's your head today?"

"It's fine. Stopped bleeding at last. I slept well, considering. I had four hours of sleep, I think."

"Good. We'll check back around lunchtime, if that's okay with you?"

"Of course. I hope you find what you're searching for."

Sara smiled and nodded. "So do we."

He closed the door. It wasn't until they were ten to fifteen feet from the door that Carla spoke. "Find what you're searching for? Did he say that?"

"Yeah, you think he was wrong to say it?"

"Why didn't he mention his kids' names?"

"Maybe his head is still playing tricks on him. Give him a break, Carla."

Her partner hitched up a shoulder. "Okay. I just think it sounded odd and wanted to point it out."

"Noted. Let's visit the school, see if anyone saw anything down there."

"Okay." Carla slumped into the seat next to her.

"Are you all right?"

"Yep, all hunky-dory from where I'm sitting."

Sara decided to let her stew for a while, she was clearly upset about something. "I think we'll get more people covered if we split up when we get there."

"I agree."

The primary school was situated in the centre of the village. Sara drew up outside, and they exited the car. Sara pushed open the large gate and entered the playground. On one side was a designated area for hopscotch and the other was laid out as a basketball court.

"How times have changed. I'm not sure I knew what basketball was when I was a kid?" Sara said.

"What a load of rubbish, the Harlem Globetrotters have been going since my parents were kids, you must have heard of them."

"Er…okay, so I lied, shoot me." Sara chuckled, pressed the buzzer and waited for a voice giving them the go-ahead to enter. She pushed open the main door which led into a hallway decorated with hundreds of kids' drawings and paintings.

At the end was a reception desk. A brunette woman in her fifties was seated behind a desk, typing at her computer. She had headphones on, and Sara had to wave to get her attention.

Blushing, the woman approached the desk. "I'm so sorry, once I get involved in something…anyway, enough of that. What can I do for you?"

"No need to apologise." Sara flashed her warrant card. "DI Sara Ramsey. Would it be possible to speak to the headmistress or headmaster?"

"Oh yes, Mrs Pringle has been expecting someone from the police to show up. I'll let her know that you're here."

"Thanks."

The woman waddled off and knocked on a door about twenty feet behind her. She went inside the room then emerged, accompanied by a woman of a similar age dressed in a black suit with a white blouse, a large bow draping at her neckline.

"Hello there. Would you like to come through to the office? Sally, can you organise some drinks? I'm sure the officers would like one."

"I will. Tea or coffee, ladies?" the chubby woman asked.

"Coffee, milk with one sugar for both of us, that's very kind of you."

"I'll bring them in. Tea for you, Mrs Pringle?"

"Yes, please."

The three of them entered the larger than average office. In the corner of the room was a Chesterfield couch and single armchair.

"Let's sit here, it'll be more comfortable. I have to ask, any news on the Jenkinson children yet?" Mrs Pringle asked.

"Thanks, it looks comfy. Nothing so far."

Mrs Pringle shook her head and sat in the armchair. Carla took out her notebook and sat next to Sara on the couch.

"Dreadful situation. After what happened to their mother yesterday as well. She worked here, you know, Gillian. Only part-time, but nevertheless, she was a valued member of our staff, and everyone is rather subdued today as their thoughts remain with her husband at this sad time. Who is behind this, do you know?"

Hmm...that's news to us. Had we known we could have questioned the staff earlier. "I wish we did. No, we're still trying to ascertain who would do such a thing. Mr Jenkinson is absolutely beside himself up at the farm."

"I have no doubt about that. We've never had anything of this magnitude happen in the village before, everyone is talking about it. If you need people to help with the search, I know you'll have dozens of volunteers."

"That sounds great. The officers at the station were out here in force last night. With no leads to go on, it proved to be a thankless expedition."

"Do you seriously think the children are still in the area, or are you on the lookout for someone who possibly drove through the village on the off chance or possibly with the intention of taking some children, any children?"

"I don't think that's the case. We believe it's linked to what happened to the children's mother, it has to be, given what we've learned so far."

"Oh, may I ask what that consists of? Or can't you say?"

"We'd rather not disclose that at this time. What sort of person was Gillian?"

A smile appeared, and Mrs Pringle's eyes welled with tears. "I suppose you'd say the best sort of person you could possibly wish to know. She didn't deserve to die in such a freak accident. That is what it was, wasn't it?"

"We're unsure at present. We're working on that for now, but until the post-mortem results confirm something different, then yes, we're classing it as an unfortunate accident. Unless you have suspicion to think differently."

"Not really. You hear so many horror stories nowadays, I suppose I have a suspicious mind and always think negatively in these circumstances. Not that I've heard of many cars exploding like that over the years. I asked my husband, he used to be a mechanic with Rolls-Royce, and he couldn't place an occasion when he'd heard of something similar occurring. It's all rather strange, isn't it?"

"In the past few months, had Gillian voiced any personal concerns with you?"

"I can't think of a time we had a conversation of that nature, no. May I ask what you mean by that?"

"Any personal problems, things wrong at home, that sort of thing."

"No, not in the slightest. I have to add that we only really discussed issues regarding work matters. If you speak to the other members of staff, they might have a different story to tell. I tend to steer clear of the staff's personal affairs, unless it affects their work. There were no problems with Gillian in that respect."

"Would it be possible for us to speak to the other members of staff this morning, while we're here?"

"Of course. In fact, I categorically give you my blessing, if you think it will help your investigation." Sally appeared with their drinks and set them on the coffee table between the chairs. "Thank you, Sally. Tell Jeanette I won't be long."

"Will do, Mrs Pringle."

"Sorry, I have another appointment soon. One of the parents has just split from her husband. We're about to discuss the security measures we have in place for such instances. A tad bizarre, given why you're here today."

"No problem, we shouldn't take up too much of your time. What about the children, Tammy and Ben, are they happy kids?"

"Yes, they're adorable, no bother at all. Do they know about their mother?"

"We don't think so. We're under the impression that Mr Jenkinson was going to leave it a few days before he told them, to let himself get used to the idea first. Such a tough call when dealing with young children."

"Indeed. I think I would've advised him to do the same if he'd asked for my advice. Now…now they're gone. It's hard to believe all this occurred in a single day. Someone must have had a rigorous plan in place, mustn't they?"

"So it would seem. A very organised plan, especially considering the amount of police and SOCO in the area at the time. Not only because of the two incidents pertaining to the Jenkinsons, but we're also conducting enquiries into the murder of one of their neighbours as well."

Mrs Pringle let out a small gasp. "No, really? Murdered you say. It's hard to imagine something as atrocious as this going on in our village. Nothing ever happens here apart from the odd school bazaar and raffle at the village hall."

"Which would suggest that an outsider is responsible for the crimes. A stranger, perhaps, or a friend of someone who lives in the village."

"My goodness, how on earth will you find out, if that's the case?"

"It'll be difficult, but we'll do it. I have every confidence in my team. If we can move on to how the children went missing… Have you heard any gossip maybe about that incident?"

"No, all I heard was that Victor Wainwright was the one who found Danny after the children had been taken. He told a member of our staff, Helen Rogers, that he found Danny lying injured in the country lane. He was driving past and pulled over to see if he was all right. As far as I know, I think Danny was said to be bleeding from a wound to his head. He was distraught, grabbed poor Victor around the throat, threatened him that if he'd harmed his kids that he would kill him. Victor was mortified by the accusation and explained to Danny that all he'd been doing was driving past at the time. There was no sign of the kids. Danny broke down in tears, said they'd gone. His whole life had been destroyed in less than twelve hours after Gillian had been blown up…" Mrs Pringle's voice faltered, and she coughed to clear her throat. "I'm sorry, I promised myself that I wouldn't shed another tear today. It's all too sad to contemplate, isn't it? To my mind, the Jenkinsons have been brutally targeted, and now those poor children are at risk. I know the police are doing their best, but is it truly going to be enough?"

"We believe whoever has abducted the children is long gone with them now. Our job from this moment forward is to try and piece things together, and quickly, bearing in mind that their lives are in danger. Someone in this village must have seen something; a stranger hanging around, possibly outside the school, ready to pounce. Or perhaps a strange car driving through the village around the time the kids were taken."

"As to the first part of your question, I can assure you we have strict security measures in place to prevent anyone from just showing up and taking a fancy to one of the children, you know what I mean. We're living in times of depravity. The number of paedophiles living amongst us is supposed to be at an all-time high level. I believe it's the school's responsibility to ensure each child in this building is the safest they can possibly be. As proven yesterday, if a stranger did try to tempt them away from the school, they failed as the abduction took place elsewhere, away from the school premises."

"You're to be admired, Mrs Pringle, I wish every school in the area was as attentive as you are."

"I pride myself on looking after the kids while they're on the premises. We have CCTV in place plus other security measures that I'd rather keep secret, if it's all the same to you."

"It's nice to see you have secure measures in place to keep the kids safe. Talking of which, would it be possible for us to view the CCTV footage around the time the kids left school yesterday? Just in case it highlights a car passing by that we should be made aware of, shall we say?"

"Of course. Gosh, I never even thought about that. I can ask Sally to sort that out for you right away." She rose from her seat and left the room, returning a few moments later. "All done. I've told her to drop what she was doing and to concentrate her efforts on obtaining that information for you before you leave."

"That really is kind of you. Interviewing the staff might help us form a bigger picture of what was going on with the Jenkinson family before Gillian was taken from us."

"Of course. I can arrange for the staffroom to be made available for you. Fortunately, we have a couple of teachers who can stand in at a moment's notice on site today. They're in the process of preparing things for the Harvest Festival in a few weeks."

"That would be excellent. We really appreciate any help you can give us. The sooner we speak to these people the better. Also, I don't suppose you know where Victor Wainwright lives, do you? We'll need to take down his statement of the events as well."

"I can definitely find that information out for you. Why don't you get on with the interviews, and I'll do some digging for you, how's that?"

"Wonderful. Thank you so much, Mrs Pringle."

"It's my pleasure. Would you like to finish your drinks first? Or are you eager to get on with things?"

Sara and Carla downed their drinks in a few mouthfuls.

"Does that answer your question?" Sara asked.

"You needn't have done that. Give me five minutes to get things organised." Mrs Pringle left the room again.

During her absence, Sara rang Will's mobile. "Will, I need you to visit Victor Wainwright, he lives in the village. I have someone trying to track his address down, but maybe call at the village shop, they're bound to know."

"Rightio, boss. Any reason you want me to visit him?"

"Apparently, he was the one who found Danny lying in the road. We need to find out what else he saw. Maybe a stranger running, a car he didn't recognise, anything and everything he can tell us at this point would be advantageous."

"I'll get on it now. Want me to take a statement while I'm there or tell him to expect someone later?"

"Let's leave that to uniform to chase up in a few days."

"Will do."

Sara ended the call. "I hope he can tell us something, if not…"

"Either Victor or the CCTV should give us a hint, surely. Like you say, if neither of those turn out to be fruitful, where does that leave us?"

"I'd rather not think about that," Sara replied, a sudden wave of nausea rippling through her.

"Are you all right? The colour just drained from your cheeks."

"Weary but otherwise fine, except for a sickly feeling in my stomach. Don't tell me this case isn't affecting you like that?"

Carla shrugged and seemed embarrassed. "Sorry, it's not. Maybe because I don't have an affinity towards children, I don't know."

"Ouch! You're a harsh woman deep down, Carla Jameson."

"Sorry, I shouldn't have told you that."

"Don't be daft. I won't think any less of you knowing that. We all have our little idiosyncrasies to deal with."

Carla smirked. "You're such an understanding boss."

"I have my moments."

Five minutes later, and Mrs Pringle breezed into the room again. "All sorted. Do you wish to view the footage first?"

"That would be great. Thank you for being so generous with your time in accommodating us at short notice."

"My pleasure. Always keen to help the police, you never know when you're likely to need their services in the future."

"I wish everyone lived by that. Sadly, the odd few don't appreciate the work we do."

She winked and tapped the side of her nose. "I bet they have secrets to hide."

Sara chuckled. "More than likely. I have to say, it always raises our suspicions, so they have to be pretty cute to get away with putting up the barriers. Anyway, that's another conversation entirely."

Sara and Carla followed Mrs Pringle back to the reception area where Sally was waiting to hit the button for them.

"If you wouldn't mind doing the honours, Sally?" Mrs Pringle said.

The receptionist nodded and prodded the Enter key.

"We've highlighted the time when the kids were leaving school, I hope that's okay?" Mrs Pringle added.

"Yes, that's fine. Ah, there's Danny now, waiting at the gates." Sara noted that he kept his distance from the other parents all gathered and nattering amongst themselves. She accepted his choice, given the turmoil he must have been in yesterday after his wife's death.

She watched his two children run into his arms. They couldn't have been happier to have seen him, which set Sara's heart fluttering. He clearly loved his children very much, any fool could see that. So why had they heard differently?

"That's touching," Carla murmured in her ear.

Sara turned and spotted the cynicism in her tone. She frowned at her partner who gave a little shrug. Sara's attention was drawn back to the screen. She focused on the traffic going past the school, particularly homing in on those cars not carrying any passengers. There weren't any, which was disappointing. "Want to speed it up a little, Sally? Everyone appears to be dispersing now. What I'm searching for is a strange vehicle. I haven't seen anything untoward so far."

The traffic died down not long after.

"That's it," Sally announced.

"Okay, thanks for your help anyway. We'll hunt around, see if there is any more footage available in the village."

"I know the garage and the shop both have cameras up. Whether they work or are just for show, I have no idea," Sally offered.

"We'll soon find out. Thanks again."

"No problem," Mrs Pringle said. "Come with me, I've set up a table in the staffroom. It's only a small room, but I'm sure it will prove adequate for your intentions and needs."

"You're very kind."

After depositing Carla and Sara in a brightly coloured room with a tiny kitchen area off to one side, Mrs Pringle went to fetch the first person for them to interview.

"We'd better stick together as there's not a lot of room to question people separately," Sara said.

Mrs Pringle returned, accompanied by a woman of a similar age who had an air of Miss Jean Brodie about her.

"This is Marie Scott, she's been here nearly as long as the foundations of the school."

All four of them laughed.

"Hardly, Mrs Pringle. I don't think I'm that ancient, although sometimes I have to wonder, the length of time it takes me to roll out of bed in the morning these days."

"I know that feeling." Mrs Pringle nudged her colleague with an elbow. "I'll leave you to it. I've arranged the interviews in order. As soon as someone leaves, they'll tell the next in line to come and see you. You know where I am if you should need me."

"We appreciate your assistance so far, Mrs Pringle." Sara smiled at the headmistress.

"Nonsense, it's what I'm here for. I hope you obtain the information you need to bring your investigation to a swift conclusion, for all our sakes. It's a dreadful situation to have hanging over our heads."

"It is that," Mrs Scott said.

"Shall we all take a seat?" Sara asked Carla and Mrs Scott, gesturing towards the table and chairs in the centre.

"Is this going to take long?" Mrs Scott pulled out a chair and sat.

"It shouldn't do, it depends on how much information you can give us."

The woman clutched her hands together. "I fear it won't be much. I knew Gillian, of course, she worked here, after all. However, I didn't really have much to do with her. I don't think any of the teaching staff did in all honesty."

"I see. Okay, we'll play it by ear for now. Have you known her long?"

"A few years."

"Do you teach her children?"

"Yes, I've had the pleasure of teaching both of them over the past few months. They've always been little angels in my classes, eager to learn, never disruptive in any way, shape or form. I was sickened to learn what trouble they're in. My heart goes out to their father."

"I'll be sure to pass that message on to him."

"Please do. He must be going through so much at the moment, after the death of his wife, and now both his children…well, gone. Do you think there's a connection between the two crimes?"

"I think it would be foolish of us not to consider that, although we need to be cautious at present. Do you mind if we focus on the children for now?"

"Not at all. Sorry, my mouth tends to run away with me on occasion."

"No need to apologise, this is unknown territory we're bridging here, for all of us, I suspect. In the past few days or weeks, have you seen anyone hanging around the school gates? A stranger to the village perhaps?"

Mrs Scott chewed on her ruby-stained lips. "I don't think so, if I had, it hasn't registered with my old mind." She prodded at her temple.

"That's okay, it was a long shot. Is there anything you'd like to offer us at all?" Sara sensed it would be wiser to end the interview early if Mrs Scott didn't have anything to give them in the way of characterisation for Gillian and her kids.

"No, I don't think I can help you further, I'm so sorry."

"It's fine. I don't think you'll be the last person to say that today. Can you send the next one in when you leave?"

"I'd like to wish you good luck and I'll keep the children in my prayers."

"I'm sure they'd appreciate that, Mrs Scott."

"We said a mass prayer for them at assembly this morning, just so you know."

"That was nice of you all to keep them in your thoughts. I'm sure it will help to keep them safe."

"We hope so, too." She left the room, and within moments, another woman took her place in the chair.

Carla noted down the younger woman's name, Ruth Hudson.

"Hello, Ruth, there's no need for you to be nervous. We're simply here to try and obtain as much information about your colleague, Gillian Jenkinson, and her children as possible. You're aware of what's gone on, I take it?"

"Oh yes. Mrs Pringle put us in the picture as soon as we arrived this morning. I was taken aback by the news, such a lovely family they were—sorry, are. It's hard to imagine anything as vile as this happening in our area. What is the world coming to if a tiny community such as Lindley can be affected by a crime as huge as this?"

"Exactly. It's very hard to understand, hence the reason why we're here today, to obtain as much insight into the family as we can. Our aim is to get the children back home to their father ASAP. So far, we've obtained next to nothing. I'm hoping you'll be able to alter that."

"Sadly, I think you're going to be disappointed. I knew Gillian in passing, only to say good morning to—she was part-time, you see, here while the classes were being held, no chance of getting to know her. She used to do a nine-til-one shift, I believe, only a few mornings a week. At least, I think she worked those hours. I've taught her kids, though, adorable they both are, well-behaved and a pleasure to be around. My heart is broken that they should have been kidnapped in such a brutal way. You'd think kids would be safe with their father, wouldn't you? The poor man took a beating from what I can gather. My, oh my, and after losing his wife a few hours earlier. It truly beggars belief, doesn't it?"

"It does. Hard to fathom. We're doing our utmost to try and figure out how the two incidents managed to take place. From what we've learned so far, this is a quiet community."

"It is indeed. The quietest spot I've ever had the fortune of residing in, that's for sure. I said to Peter, my husband, once the news had reached us, that we should consider moving on."

"Maybe that would be a rash decision to make in the circumstances. It could be a one-off."

"A one-off? Are you saying you think this family was intentionally targeted and you believe the rest of us are safe in our beds at night?"

"That's a pretty loaded question. What I'm saying is that I don't think people should be putting their houses up for sale just yet, especially if they love the area so much. Crimes like this have a habit of catching people off-guard, but they are not that uncommon in the real world, as opposed to a tightly knit community such as Lindley."

"I suppose you're right. I've been guilty of making knee-jerk decisions in the past. My husband pointed that out to me in an unkindly manner last night."

"That's a shame, sorry to hear that. Take time to reconsider the life you have here. I'm sure you'll come to the right conclusion soon. If you have nothing else to tell us, could you send the next person in, please?"

"Oh, is that it? I'm so sorry I was so useless. Forgive me for burdening you with my problems, it wasn't intentional. I intend volunteering later, when the search party starts up again after school. It's the least we can do, isn't it? As a caring community, I mean."

"Any help in trying to find the children is a blessing in disguise. Our resources are stretched to capacity as it is."

"I'm sure. Bloody government has a lot to answer for with the cutbacks they've made to every arm of the public sector, teaching included. My husband is a fireman...sorry, don't get me started on that one. It was a pleasure speaking with you. Good luck with the rest of your investigation. Oh, do you want to give me a card, just in case I think of anything once my head has cleared a bit?"

"Of course." Sara smiled and slid the card across the desk.

After Ruth left the room, Sara let out a large sigh. "It's heartbreaking to think how much all this is affecting such a quaint, inoffensive community, isn't it?"

"I have to admit, that thought isn't at the top of my agenda."

"I know, we have the kids to think about but, ugh...ignore me. Shit! Now you've got me bloody saying it."

Carla sniggered. "I knew you would, eventually. I wish things would brighten up; we're getting nowhere fast here. Do we really need to know what angels the kids are from everyone we speak to? Aren't most kids of that age sweet and adorable?"

"It depends whose company they keep, I suppose."

The door opened, and a teary-eyed woman of around thirty-five walked in and plonked herself down heavily in the chair opposite them. "I'm sorry, I'm so upset. Gillian was my best friend. Hubby told me I should stay off work today, but I knew I'd be worse off there, having nothing better to do than think of Gillian, Tammy and Ben. Oh my, here I go again." She openly broke down in tears.

Sara left the table and went in search of a mug to fill with water. She offered it to the woman who gratefully accepted it. "Why don't you tell us your name?"

"I'm so sorry for breaking down like this. I'm Vanessa Pilkington. I'm beside myself. I feel so helpless, knowing that those kids are out there, being terrorised for all we know. Innocent children who have never done a thing wrong in their damn lives. How could anyone be as heartless as to tear them away from their grieving father like that?"

"We intend to get to the bottom of this. You say you and Gillian were best friends. Can you give us a little information about your relationship?"

"What do you mean? She meant everything to me. Her kids often stayed over at my house with Cindy and Ryan, my two, they're the same age as Tammy and Ben. Shit! Who could do such a thing? Why kidnap them? Is the same person responsible for killing their mother?"

"We're treating Gillian's death as an accident until we get the appropriate results from the pathologist telling us otherwise. So, no, we're not linking the crimes in that respect, but something that Danny highlighted yesterday has caused us great concern."

"Are you going to tell me what that is?"

"I'd rather not just yet. Maybe you can tell us if anything had occurred in Gillian's life lately that you regarded as questionable?"

"Are you referring to the notes?"

"So she told you about them. What about the ewe that was found?"

"Ewe? I don't know what you're talking about. Don't tell me someone hurt one of their flock?"

"Precisely that. I don't want to go into detail, but it wasn't nice. Going back to the notes, was Gillian upset about them?"

"Very." She sniffled and wiped her nose on a tissue.

"To what extent?"

"Just upset. It has been one thing after another this year for her and Danny."

"Care to enlighten us?"

"They were having marital problems. Money was super tight and…"

"And?" Sara probed, her interest level rising to near maximum.

"And, I really don't know whether I should tell you this or not, in light of what's happened."

"Anything you tell us will be regarded as confidential, I promise you."

She weaved her tissue through her fingers for several seconds and then glanced up at Sara. "Gillian was making plans to leave Danny. There, I've said it, put it out in the open at last. Even my husband isn't aware of that fact."

"Right. Do you know why?"

"Things had got too much for her. That's why she was having her car serviced. So she'd be able to get away should the moment arise."

"Serviced? Is that what she told you? And go where?"

"Yes, service. Are you telling me there was something wrong with her car?"

"We were told her brake line had been cut."

"Really? Oh no!"

"Where was she intending to go?"

"She has a sister up in Seascale, Cumbria. I believe she was intending to stay there for a while, until she got a job and was back on her feet again."

"Hmm…we were told she didn't have any family. So the plan was put in place, is that what you're telling me?"

"Yes."

"Was Danny aware that things had got so bad between them?"

"I think he'd sussed something was wrong. There was definitely tension there. He's…"

"He's what?" Sara's heart raced.

"I feel bad telling you this, what with the problems he's having but…I have to for Gillian's sake, although it's too late for her now." She broke down again. "Maybe if I'd spoken out earlier, she'd still be alive today."

"You're not making sense. Please, can you just tell us what you know, Vanessa?"

After a long pause, she gulped then dried her eyes again. "I failed her as a friend. My husband warned me not to interfere in their marriage. God, why didn't I listen to my gut?"

"Vanessa, what are you trying to tell us?"

"That he was a downright bully, not only to her, but those two babies as well."

"Whoa! Do you realise what you're saying?"

"Yes, it breaks my heart to utter the words, but it's the bloody truth. He used to beat her and the kids, or try to. She always put herself in harm's way to prevent the kids getting hurt."

"Okay, so they had an abusive marriage, but are you inferring that he might have killed her?"

"I don't know. I thought that at one time, but you told me that Gillian's death is being regarded as an accident. Now I'm confused."

"It is what it is, until we get things clarified by the pathologist. What about the threatening notes?"

She shrugged. "You tell me. That's another issue that doesn't sit well with me. I'm so full of hatred for him after what Gillian has divulged over the years, that I can't think further than him being the guilty one."

"Your loyalty to your friend is admirable in this instance."

"If that's what you believe this is, then fine."

"We'll delve into what you've told us. It's going to be hard to back up your claims, though."

"Why? You can question him about it. Please, keep my name out of it, won't you? He hates me enough as it is. I don't want him turning up on my doorstep causing aggro between my husband and me."

"I'll do that, don't worry. Do you have her sister's details? Name and address perhaps?"

"Yes, in my bag somewhere. Want me to get it?"

"If you wouldn't mind?"

Vanessa flew out of her chair and left the room.

"What do you make of that statement?" Carla asked the second the door shut behind the woman.

"I think it's a typical statement, coming from a best friend who obviously hates the man because of how he's treated her friend over the years. We know he's a bastard, according to his neighbours, but I'm sorry, he doesn't seem the type to rig up an explosion in his own car just so he can do away with his wife. We have to remember the threatening notes element here, also, if he was desperately short of money, why on earth would he write his own car off and not hers?"

Carla thought and ran a hand over her face. "While I agree with you, there's also the fact that her car was in the garage after the brake lines were cut? Coincidence or someone trying to kill her and failing?"

"And that someone could be the person who wrote the notes, Carla. You're also forgetting a major point here."

"I am?"

"His kids have now been kidnapped, which is our main reason for being here today."

Carla rolled her eyes and tutted. "I hadn't forgotten, I'm just trying to work through the clues people are offering. It would be careless of us to ignore what her best friend is telling us."

"I have no intention of ignoring it, all I'm saying is that we need to be cautious. I'm not prepared to go back up there and start dragging him over the coals. Ugh…none of this is making any sense, not really. Maybe having a chat with the sister will point us in the right direction."

"Maybe. I wonder if she knows about the kids. Did she and Danny get on? I'm thinking not. In that case, would he have likely called her?"

"Again, we won't know that until I ring her. Bugger, what's taking Vanessa so long?"

With that, Vanessa appeared in the open doorway. "Sorry, I got waylaid by an upset pupil wandering around the corridor. She's a friend of Tammy's. She thought she'd ask to go to the loo and try to help find Tammy while she was 'free', so to speak."

"Bless her. Is she okay? All this must be an horrendous shock for the kids."

"It is. Most of them don't really understand. She'll be fine. I called her mum to come and fetch her. She's on the way. Now, here's the information you need. I only obtained it from her last week. I knew her escape plan was imminent and didn't want her leaving without giving me her sister's details. I was desperate to stay in touch with her, even if she was considering moving hundreds of miles away."

"You were a good friend, Vanessa."

She sat and handed Carla her address book.

After writing the information in her notebook, Carla smiled at Vanessa and handed the book back to her. "Thanks, I have that now."

"Good. Is there anything else you need from me?"

"I don't think so, not unless you'd like to share any more of Gillian's dark secrets?"

"That's all I can think of at this time. I'll give you a ring if anything else comes to mind. Please, do everything you can to find Tammy and Ben."

"We will. First, we need to find the person who reportedly snatched them."

"Good luck. The villagers are going to do their best after work to try to find them. I hope it's not too late."

"You've been incredibly helpful. Is there anyone else to see now or are you the last?"

"Maureen is next. Shall I ask her to come in?"

"If you wouldn't mind."

Vanessa walked out again and was soon replaced by a petite woman of around forty-five. She was the jittery type, her hands proving distracting to Sara as she asked her the relative questions, the ones she'd asked the previous interviewees. It proved to be a waste of time speaking to the woman, she didn't really know Gillian and only taught at the school the odd day a week, when she was needed, as she was a supply teacher.

Sara completed the interview in record time. She and Carla made their way back to Mrs Pringle's office. Sally told them to go right in as she was expecting them.

"That's us finished. Many thanks to you and your staff today," Sara said.

Mrs Pringle glanced up from her paperwork and offered a weak smile. "I hope the interviews were helpful."

"A mixture. We have a few leads to pick up on. Thanks for sparing us the time today."

"My pleasure. Will you keep me informed? Sorry, I couldn't find an address for Victor."

"Don't worry, we'll locate him. I'll keep you posted on what we find out."

Sara and Carla left the main entrance.

Sara took a moment to study the area. "If this is the main street, someone must have seen either a stranger lingering or a strange car in the vicinity yesterday."

"Yeah, but who? I bet we don't find out until the press conference is aired. So annoying, as we need to know now. I dread to think what's happening to those kids at this moment."

Sara shook her head. "I'm doing my best not to think about that, Carla, I suggest you do the same. This investigation is proving to be hard enough as it is without having that added pressure bearing down on us."

"What next?"

"We need to follow the CCTV route and request the footage from any of the shops. Not that there are many, there's only the one from what I can see. A general store and post office rolled into one. First, you've just reminded me to chase up Jane, see if she's managed to arrange the conference. I would've thought she'd have rung me by now." She fished out her mobile and rang the press officer.

"Damn, I knew I had to do something. Sorry, Sara, I got ambushed by my boss about something. I would've got back to you eventually."

"Hey, no worries. Is it today?"

"Yes, at four. I hope that suits you?"

"It does. Thanks, Jane, you're an angel."

"I'll be there to hold your hand, should you need it."

"That's reassuring. See you later."

"You will."

Carla had wandered off but was still within a few feet of her. "What are you thinking?"

"Do we know the exact point where the kids were taken?"

Sara pointed up the road. "Somewhere up there. Why?"

"Just trying to work things out in my head, that's all."

"And what conclusion have you come to?"

"Nothing much. Only that if the incident occurred not long after school was finished for the day, there would have been dozens of people milling around here and that someone must have seen something. Why hasn't that person come forward?"

"Pure speculation, that's why? Without evidence to back up that likely scenario, we're screwed."

Carla frowned. "I don't get it. It doesn't add up, no matter which way I try to assess it."

"Hang in there. It seems to me there are too many variables for us to consider at this stage, and none of it is making any sense. The only aspect we're sure of is that the kids have gone missing. Good news on the conference, it's planned for four this afternoon. That gives us plenty of time to speak to more people before we have to head back to base."

"Good. I'm thinking we need to start shaking some trees. We've got all this evidence and nothing to show for it, as such."

"All this evidence? Hardly! What have we got? Two threatening notes which we suspect have possibly led to the death of Gillian. We've got nothing whatsoever on poor Frank's death."

"Don't forget his money was missing, we can't discount that aspect, so we could be dealing with an opportunistic burglar, chancing his arm, knowing that SOCO and the police were within spitting distance of the farm."

"Yeah, that's another thing that jars with me. Would someone truly risk being caught like that?"

"I hear you. I need to ring Will, see if he's tracked down Victor Wainwright."

"Wouldn't he have got back to you if he had?"

"Possibly. I'll try him anyway."

"Why don't I see if the shopkeeper has anything to offer?" Sara nodded and Carla marched towards the shop, a hundred feet or more from their position.

Sara punched in her colleague's number. "Hi, Will, can you talk?"

"Just finishing up the interview now, boss. I'll give you a call back in two minutes, if that's all right?"

"Fine with me." Sara ended the call and walked towards the shop. True to his word, Will rang back within two minutes.

"Sorry about that, boss. I'm glad you rang, though, gave us an excuse to get out of there. You know how lonely old folks get. Desperate for a chat to put the world to rights, he was."

"Oops, sorry to burden you with that, Will. What did he have to say?"

"He saw a red, what he describes as a 'gas guzzler', driving up the hill not long before he found Jenkinson."

"Excellent news. If he was that observant, tell me he got the make of the vehicle and the plate number? Otherwise, we're fucked."

"Then we're fucked, well and truly—he couldn't tell me either of those, boss. Sorry. Almost two hours Barry and I have been sat in that house, and when he finally got around to mentioning the crime, that's all he had to offer."

"Shit! What a frigging time-waster. How accurate do you think his account is?"

"Barry and I have our doubts. You should've heard some of the drivel that came out of his mouth. He reverted back to being a private in the army at one point. Frightened the shit out of me when he shot out of his chair and stood to attention."

Sara chuckled. "Ah, the bloody downside of getting old. Does he live alone?"

"Yes, he has carers who visit him a few times during the day. One showed up while he was talking to us. He sent her away, told her he was far too busy to deal with her."

"Oh dear, poor woman. I hope she wasn't too offended."

"No, I had a quick word with her before she left the house. She laughed it off, told me it was a regular occurrence and she was used to him by now. Tell you what, though, it made me doubt the information he's given us. It could be completely made up for all we know."

"Hang on, if that's the case, and if he's that bad, should he still be driving?"

"I was wondering the same. Want me to look into it? I'd hate him to cause an accident. I'd feel guilty knowing that I should have stopped it."

"Yes, it's worth making a call to the doctor and a follow-up call to DVLA, if he's that bad."

"I seriously think he is."

"Then do it. I'd rather not put too much emphasis on the information he gave you for now, then, just in case. Let's stick to the facts we can back up with hard evidence, as in camera footage, rather than take his word which is dubious to say the least."

"I'm with you on that front. Anything else you want us to do?"

"Where are you? What part of the village?"

"At the top end."

"Okay, head back this way and start knocking on some doors. Someone must have seen something. I refuse to leave this village until we've knocked on every single door."

"As you wish."

Sara said goodbye and entered the shop. Carla was at the far end studying camera footage with the owner of the store.

"Any luck?"

Her partner briefly glanced up and shook her head. "Nothing as yet, just like the school footage."

"That's regrettable. Keep searching. We might be looking for a red 'gas guzzler'. Don't ask, that's all we have to go on so far."

"Frustrating."

"And some," Sara replied. She surveyed the interior of the shop. "Have you been here long? Sorry, I'm DI Sara Ramsey."

The shopkeeper smiled. "I'm Kat Davis. I've owned the shop for around fifteen years. We've never had to deal with anything like this before. Two children going missing plus two deaths, all on the same day. I have to say, everyone I've spoken to this morning has been in shock."

"It is very perplexing. Do you know the family, the Jenkinsons?"

"Yes, her more than him. Gillian worked at the school and often popped in after picking the kids up to buy them a bag of sweets. She was such a pleasure to deal with, patient, and she cherished her kids."

"It is a very sad case. We're doing our very best to try to determine what happened to the children but we've hit several brick walls in the process."

"I don't envy you, that's for sure. If there's anything I can do to help, you only have to ask."

"Maybe put a sign up on your counter, telling your customers to ring the station if they have any information for us. There's going to be a press conference later today, hopefully that will jog people's memories."

"I'm surprised no one has come forward so far."

"May I ask why?"

She smiled. "Shall we say we have a few nosey parkers in our midst?"

"Ah, village gossips, where would we be without them?" Sara sniggered.

"Wait, what's that?" Carla's head shot up, and she pointed at the screen.

Sara raced to stand beside her and peered over her shoulder while Kat rewound the CD.

"There. A red 'gas guzzler'. Isn't it a Nissan Qashqai? The old man probably implies all large cars of this ilk are in that category."

A tsunami of adrenaline whooshed through Sara. "You're right. Is it possible to get a plate number?"

Kat went back and forth a few times. "No, it's impossible to make out. Wait a minute, why don't you go and see old Ron at the garage? There's not a lot he doesn't know about the cars in this village, maybe he'll be able to give you more information about it."

"We'll do that. Thanks, Kat. You've been most helpful. I don't suppose you can make us a copy of the CD, can you?"

"Afraid I wouldn't know how. I'll ask Andy, my husband, to do it when he gets back from the cash and carry."

"Marvellous," Sara shouted from the doorway.

Outside, it was Carla who led the way to the garage. "It's over here."

"I can't believe it, at last, we have something to cling on to."

"I wouldn't go getting too excited just yet."

With Carla's warning ringing in her ears, Sara upped her pace.

9

*R*on Harris turned out to be a very wise old man. "Yep, I know the exact car you're talking about. He came in here yesterday and filled up."

"Did he pay by cash?"

Ron shook his head slowly. "Nope, by card. Want me to dig the receipt out for you?"

Sara's hand slapped against her chest. "If you would, this could be the lead that cracks this case."

"Really? Well, I'd better get my finger out then. I was bloody shocked to learn about those two kiddies. I knew Gillian, their mother, fine woman she was, very friendly. Always stopped to chat with me. There aren't many around here who are prepared to do that, I can tell you."

"It's very sad she's no longer with us. Even sadder that the children are missing. However, this proof you have for us could prove crucial in getting them back." She held up her tightly crossed fingers.

"Here you are, I told you I'd find it for you. I'll run a copy off, I have a small printer in the office. You understand I can't give you the original, the accountant would have my knackers as a paperweight if I did that."

"I get that. A copy will suffice, thanks."

The man slipped behind his counter and out the back.

Sara lightly punched Carla's arm, her excitement mounting. "This could be it."

"I'd keep a lid on that enthusiasm if I were you, we still have to locate the damn vehicle. It could be anywhere by now. Whoever has the kids is hardly going to stay in the area, are they?"

"Okay, thanks for bursting my bubble. I'd rather keep thinking positively about things, if you don't mind. Those kids are relying on us. Thinking negatively isn't going to help, partner."

"All I was suggesting was for you not to get too carried away with this. We still need to find the driver. That could take days. Depending on his agenda, the kids could be on their way in a container lorry or tucked up on a cargo ship by now."

Sara raised her hand. "No, I refuse to contemplate either of those suggestions, Carla. I must insist we remain positive on this one."

"All right, but it'll be against my better judgement."

Ron returned, putting an end to their conversation. "There you go, I've stuck it in an envelope for you. Generous of me, eh?"

"Very. Thanks so much, Ron. Is there anything else you can think of that we might be interested in?"

"Such as?"

"To do with the family perhaps?"

"Not really. The garage in the next village told me they were mending Gillian's car. Seems odd that her brake line had been cut, don't you think?"

"It's something we're looking into at present, along with a number of other leads. Our priority remains with finding the children, though."

"Oh, I wholeheartedly agree that should be the case. Those kids will be scared out of their tiny little minds. Sweet kids, great manners, considering."

"Considering what?"

"Who their father is. Let's just say he's not a pleasant person to be around. I've had more than a few run-ins with him."

"In connection with what?"

"Wanting to run up a tab for his fuel. Bloody cheek, as if I haven't got overheads of my own to meet. I'm not a charity, I told him as much, too. Of course, he got the hump about that. Gillian always felt the need to apologise for his behaviour. It was nothing to do with her, he's the one with the problem, it was never her. Sad to see her go, she'll be sorely missed around here, you can take my word for that."

"We've heard similar tales about both of them. Are you aware that they were being threatened?"

He staggered back against the counter. "Never. Who by?"

"We're unsure at present. All I'm saying is that maybe there were extenuating circumstances for his behaviour. His mood swings perhaps. If he was being threatened, he'd be inclined to be more guarded about strangers, wouldn't he?"

"You're not as silly as you look. Sorry, that was uncalled for, it's just one of my little sayings."

Sara waved away his apology. "It's worth considering."

"It is. Okay, I take back some of what I said, however, not all of it. He still didn't have the right to ask for an account to be opened up for him. People in this village should use this garage more instead of going into the main towns to fill up at the supermarket garages. There's no way I can compete with their damn prices, no way, I tell you. Folks in small villages need to appreciate what they've got because one day I might pack it all in, and then where will they be?"

"The struggle is real, I can imagine. We're going to head off now and try to find this person. You didn't recognise him at all?"

"Nope. A total stranger, he was."

Sara browsed the forecourt before she asked if he could describe the man. "Wait! What about the CCTV footage?"

He clicked his thumb and forefinger together. "Damn, I should have thought about that. Too concerned with those kiddies to think straight, that's my problem. Just a tick."

He flicked the 'open' sign on the door to 'closed' and invited them into a small back room. "There are a couple of seats buried under that lot if you want to shove all that on the floor. This shouldn't take long. I've got the time I need on the credit card receipt. Now then…if only I could remember how to work the damn machine." He winked at them. "I'm joshing you. Here we go, this should work if I press this button here."

And it did. The red car instantly appeared on the screen, and a man in his late thirties to early forties got out to fill up his vehicle.

"Can you fast forward to when he leaves?"

Ron pressed a key and paused it the second the car drove off. He zoomed the camera in to the number plate, and Sara and Carla both let out a "yes" at the same time.

"Is it possible to get a copy? I'll take a photo on my phone for now, but we'll need proper evidence for when it goes to court."

"Can you leave it with me a few days? My son is a whizz with this sort of thing. Me, I'm well out of my depth."

"I thought as much, no disrespect. You've worked wonders so far, and we appreciate your help, Ron."

He beamed, and his cheeks flushed. "Get away with you, it's all part of the service, ladies."

Sara snapped the footage on her mobile, thanked Ron again and left the garage shop faster than a speeding train. "God, I'm so thrilled about this breakthrough."

Carla tutted. "Are you going to jump up and down for joy all day or call it in?"

"On the case now." She rang the station and spoke to Christine, giving her as many details as she had to hand.

Christine let out a whoop. "I've got it. Terry Abbott, he lives in Bromyard. Oh shit!"

"What is it?" Sara asked, her stomach muscles clenching at the tone of her colleague's voice.

"He's got a record."

"For what?"

"Kiddie fiddling," Christine replied.

"Fuck. Just what I didn't want to hear. Give me the bloody address, Christine."

Carla wrote the address down in her notebook as Sara repeated it.

Sara ended the call and immediately dialled another number. "Hi,

Will, meet us at the garage in the main street. We've got a hit on a possible suspect."

"We're on our way."

Sara paced the garage forecourt until she saw her two colleagues running towards them. "Where's your car?"

Will breathlessly pointed behind her. "That direction, I think, I've lost my bearings."

"It is," Barry chipped in. "Is the suspect local, boss?"

"Bromyard, not too far. We'll all go and pick him up. Providing he's there, of course. Carla, I should have thought about the time—ring Christine back once we're in the car, see where he works, just in case he's not at home."

The four of them dashed in different directions to retrieve their cars. Will drew up alongside them a few minutes later.

"He should be there. According to Christine, he doesn't have a job. How he manages to run an expensive car is anybody's business."

"We'll follow you, boss," Will called out.

Sara selected first gear and drove up the hill towards Bromyard. "God, I hope he's there and not keeping the kids locked away at a secret location."

"Think positively." Carla grinned.

"Smartarse. I am, honest."

"It didn't sound like it to me. They'll be there, they have to be, he hasn't had time to shift them, not yet."

"How do you know? For all we know he might have had a rendezvous with someone and palmed the kids off onto them within hours of them being snatched."

"Do you think that's how he got the money for his swanky car? By abducting kids and selling them to the highest bidder?"

"Let's draw the line at speculating about it until we track him down."

10

$\mathcal{J}$erry Abbott's red Qashqai was parked outside his terraced house. Sara and Carla high-fived each other and then exited the vehicle. Will and Barry remained seated in their car, as instructed—first sign of trouble, and they would be called upon.

"Here we go. Are you ready for this?"

"What, grilling a paedo?"

"If you put it like that...ugh, I hope I can keep my temper under control. We both have to, those kids' lives are at stake."

"I know. Does that mean we can let loose once they've been found?"

"We'll see." Sara winked and pushed open the dilapidated wooden gate. By the look of things, the garden was the local dumping ground for litter louts. "God, how can anyone put up with seeing this ruddy mess every day and not do anything about it?"

Carla shook her head and reached out to ring the bell. She wiped her finger on her trousers after touching it. "Yuck! Looks like bloody snot on there. Ever wished you hadn't done something without putting latex on first?" she whispered.

"Many a time. I can hear someone whistling on the other side."

The door opened to reveal a balding, rotund man, sporting a Manchester United shirt with stains down the front.

Sara had her warrant card ready in her hand and shoved it in the man's bewildered face.

"Thought they'd send women this time to harass me, eh? You can't keep showing up here like this. I'm going to get my solicitor to have a word with your superiors if this continues."

"If you'd care to calm down, Mr Abbott, we have a few questions for you."

"About what? No, wait, let me guess…a frigging kid has gone missing, and you think I've had something to do with it, right?"

"Spot on. Actually, two children from the same family."

His face contorted with rage, and his cheeks reddened. "What the fuck! No way am I guilty of this. The doctor has me on tablets…you know, to suppress any urges I might have had in the past. I'm over that now. I haven't been near a kid in God knows how long."

"Then you won't mind accompanying us to the station then, will you?"

"Yes, damn right I'd mind. I've told you why. I ain't done anything wrong, I swear I ain't."

"Get your coat. You're coming with us."

He tried to slam the door in their faces, but Sara stuck her foot in the way and Carla shoved the door open, pinned him up against the wall in the hallway and slapped her cuffs on him within a few frantic seconds.

Barry and Will appeared behind Sara.

"Everything all right, boss?" Will asked.

"I think Carla has everything in hand. Take him back to the station, boys."

Abbott protested his innocence as Will and Barry marched him out to their car and placed him in the back.

"Are you all right?" Sara asked.

"I'm fine. Never enjoyed slapping cuffs on a man so much before. Shall we have a look around while we're here?"

Sara led the way. "We might as well. I know we're supposed to get a warrant, but these are exceptional circumstances, and he willingly opened the door and invited us in, didn't he?"

"He did." Carla smirked. "I'll take upstairs."

"Search everywhere. Have you got some gloves on you?"

Carla withdrew a pair from her pocket and snapped them on. "Never go anywhere without them."

They both laughed.

"Too much information."

Carla ran up the stairs, and Sara wandered through the tiny house, her gut telling her that the property wasn't the right one, not to tuck two kids away anyway. That thought didn't prevent her opening every cupboard and searching behind every piece of furniture filling the downstairs rooms. Nothing. Tammy and Ben were nowhere to be seen.

"Anything up there?" she called up to Carla.

"Nope, except a bloody smelly mess, dirty washing littering the floor of the main bedroom, and unpacked boxes filling the back bedroom. I've checked the wardrobe and under the bed. Wish I hadn't done that, dozens of mugs under there, chock-full of mould." Carla heaved, coming down the stairs to join her.

"Poor you. In all honesty, I wasn't really expecting to find them here."

"So, where are they? I hope we're not too late. Maybe he's part of a paedophile ring and the kids are kept elsewhere, but where?"

"We'd better get back to the station and start grilling him about that. Time's getting on. I've got an hour or so to get the information out of him before I have to go in front of the cameras."

"I don't envy you that task."

Sara closed the front door, and they got in the car. Will pulled out behind them, and they parked the vehicles in the station car park around thirty minutes later.

Sara groaned, "Half an hour now."

"Shit! Let's hope he's the talkative type. The solicitor should be here by now. When I forewarned them that we were on our way, they said they'd send someone right away."

"Thanks for that. The odds on him divulging everything from the get-go...well, I won't be banking on it."

"PMA."

Will and Barry accompanied Abbott to Interview Room One. Sara stopped off to ask Jeff if the duty solicitor had arrived yet. He gestured to a man sitting behind her, reading through a notebook.

"Thanks. What's his name?"

"Mr Lancett."

Sara turned and approached the man. "Mr Lancett, we're ready to go when you are. I'm DI Sara Ramsey."

"I'm all fit, ready for action as they say. I take it that was my client who just passed through here?"

"Correct. He's proclaiming his innocence. We have reason to believe we have the right man. Just to warn you, I have a press conference I need to attend at four regarding the case, so I'm hoping to crack on straight away, no softly-softly on this one."

"I understand. Let's play things by ear, shall we?"

Sara motioned for him to join her. She entered her code into the security door.

Carla, Will, Barry and Abbott were the only people in the room.

"Will and Barry, would you mind guarding the door outside? Otherwise things are going to be a bit tight in here for all of us," Sara said.

Her two colleagues nodded and left the room. Mr Lancett, Carla and Sara all took their seats, and Carla gave the necessary information to the machine to get the interview underway.

"Mr Abbott—all right if I call you Terry?" Sara asked.

"Do what you like, your lot usually do," Abbott retorted spikily.

"Okay, Terry, can you tell us where you were between the hours of three and four yesterday afternoon?"

Abbott's brow furrowed, and his eyes narrowed. "You tell me."

Sara exhaled. "I put it to you that you were driving through Lindley village. May I ask why?"

"Oh yeah, that's right. No reason."

"Did you make a stop in the village?"

"Yeah, to fill up."

"To put petrol in your car, is that correct?"

"Yeah, I just told you that." He turned to his solicitor and leaned over. "Is there a law against that nowadays?"

"Not as far as I know. Is there, Inspector?" Mr Lancett queried.

"No. Give me time, I'm getting there. After you filled up with petrol or diesel, what did you do then?"

"I continued on my journey, couldn't wait to get out of there."

"Any particular reason?"

His gaze darted between her and Carla. "Because the kids were coming out of school."

"And that bothered you?"

"It might have done a few years ago, not since I started taking the suppressants. I still try to avoid coming into contact with them, just in case."

"Why?"

"I just do."

"What you're really telling us is that the urges are still there, aren't they?"

He removed his cuffed hands from his lap and put them on the table in front of him. "Maybe, but I didn't do what you've dragged me in here for. I swear. Don't go blaming me just because I drove through that bloody village. It was a one-off, first time I've been through there. My tank was running on empty, and I saw a sign for the garage on the main road so took a detour."

"In that case, why didn't you continue on your journey by just going back the way you came?"

"You want the truth?" His gaze latched on to hers.

"It's always advisable to tell the truth in these circumstances, Terry."

"I freaked out when the bloody kids started coming out of school. I hadn't expected that. I'd lost track of time. In all fairness, I didn't even know there was a bloody school in the village. I was shocked when I saw the little ones…"

"Shocked or excited?"

"Shocked," he sneered. "Look, you mentioned two kids going missing. You're wasting your time asking me about them, I know nothing. And you know what? You should be out there searching for them not grilling me."

"We are, don't worry. Why shouldn't we suspect you of having anything to do with their disappearance?"

"I told you why, I'm on medication. Would you be interrogating me if I'd had my dick chopped off instead? No, I didn't think so. The medication does the same thing, it stops the urges, the dangerous thoughts from entering my head. If you don't believe me, ask my doctor. Sod it, ask any doctor worth their weight in gold. They'll all tell you the same. You have to believe me."

Sara raised a finger. "It's all very well you saying that, but what it boils down to is whether you've been taking the medication or not."

"Why wouldn't I?"

"Why would you? It must become a chore, having to down half a dozen pills every day, mustn't it?"

"It's two pills. See, you know nothing. All you've set out to do is pin this on me. I'm telling you for the third time, I haven't touched any damn kids, not in years. Before I went down for it the last time. Do you have any idea how men like me are treated in the nick? They're unforgiving, the other cons."

"They detest paedophiles, is that what you're telling me?"

"Yeah, there's a special wing for them in most prisons, but the one I was in was full. So I was forced to live amongst the other crims, the hard-nosed ones. I got bashed up, set upon, more times than I care to remember. It did the trick, well, that and the medication. I won't go near another kid, ever, I swear I won't. I was threatened by a mob inside that if I ever touched another kid they'd come after me. I've had several visits from the gang since I got out, to ensure I live up to my promise. You see, that's why I told you you've got the wrong person. You need to get out there, find those kids and stop hounding me just because I've got a record. That record means fuck all, I swear."

"That's quite a speech, Terry."

"It's the truth. Make of it what you will, but don't hang the blame for this around my neck, got that?"

"Let's study the evidence. We've got a known paedophile taking a shortcut through a village he's never stepped foot in before and, by coincidence, two small children go missing around the same time. You can see why I'm inclined to go with the evidence rather than what you've just told me, can't you?"

"No. You're fitting me up. Big time. I've done nothing wrong."

"What have you done with the children?" Sara persisted, convinced more than ever she had the right man in custody, despite him pleading his innocence.

"I don't have them," he shouted, his temper rising. "Why won't you believe me?" he added, his voice softening.

"I've explained how I've come to the conclusion you're involved. What are you doing now, selling them?"

"Are you crazy? You have no proof and yet you insist on pointing the finger at me." He nudged the solicitor with his elbow. "Can't you do something about her? She's on the wrong track. I ain't taken the kids. Tell her."

"My client has a point, Inspector. The only evidence you have is that he was innocently driving through the village and stopped off to fill up his car at the local garage. Forgive me if I'm wrong, but how does that constitute a crime?"

Sara pinched the bridge of her nose and glanced at her watch. She had ten minutes left to obtain a confession. "Look, if you tell us where they are or who has them now, we'll offer you some kind of plea bargain."

Abbott laughed and tipped his head back. "Have you heard yourself? Let me say this again, I've done absolutely nothing wrong since I came out of prison two years ago."

"Do you work?"

"What's that got to do with anything?"

"You have a brand-new car sitting outside your home, and yet your house is a tip, which signifies to me that you're at home all day."

He shook his head. "Some detective you are. No, I don't work, you're right there, and the car is none of your business."

"Oh, but it is, especially if the money you handed over for it came from criminal activity. We can seize it under the Proceeds of Crime Act 2002."

He gaped, and she did an imaginary fist pump.

"No way. It was bought legitimately, I'm telling you. I've done nothing wrong."

"How did you pay for a vehicle worth what? Thirty grand or thereabouts?"

"Do I have to tell her?" Abbott demanded.

His solicitor stared at him. "No, you don't have to tell her, but if you're willing to hand over the information it will help your defence."

"My defence? In what? She can't arrest me for something I ain't done. Jesus, where do you guys get off hounding me about this, for fuck's sake? I'm innocent. I ain't been near a damn kid, how many times do I have to frigging say it?"

Sara ignored his tirade and pressed on. "The car, Terry. Where did you get the funds to purchase it?"

He huffed and puffed and turned to his solicitor again, who raised his eyebrow. "I used the money I received from my inheritance."

"We'll need details regarding the will reading et cetera to corroborate the facts."

"In other words, you think I'm lying. Jesus, see, even when I tell the truth, you don't frigging believe a word I'm saying. I'll tell you what, why don't I sit here instead and go down the 'no comment' route? That's sure to tick you off. I can't emphasise enough that I haven't touched any kids. My being there in the village yesterday was a c-o-i-n-c-i-d-e-n-c-e. I was out for a drive and noticed the car was running low. Shit, I wish I hadn't bothered going out now. You've got nothing on me. You searched my house, I know you did, and found nothing."

"You're right, we did search the house. Which is why I suspect you're holding the children elsewhere. Now give us that address."

"What address? Jesus, how many more times do I have to tell you?" he growled through clenched teeth.

Sara glanced at her watch again. She was running late, she had two minutes before the conference began. "I have to go. DS Jameson, I'll send Will in to take over from me. You continue the interview."

Carla nodded. "Okay."

She left the room in spite of Abbott's protestations. "Will, sit in with Carla. I have to go to the conference."

"Gosh, I'd forgotten all about that. Of course, boss."

"I hadn't. Damn thing. Good luck in there."

"Ditto," Sara flung over her shoulder as she ran the length of the hallway in the direction of the press conference room.

Jane was waiting at the door for her. "Talk about cutting it fine. Are you trying to cause me a heart attack?"

"Sorry, I was tied up, interviewing a suspect."

"For this investigation?"

Sara held up her fingers. "Yes, but let's forge ahead with the conference anyway. He's denying he has anything to do with it."

"Ugh... not good. We should get in there and take a seat."

Sara brushed her black suit down and straightened her back as she entered the room full of her least favourite people, journalists. *Shark-infested waters ahead, old girl, steady as I go.*

The next twenty minutes consisted of Sara laying out the facts, there weren't many of them, and being bombarded with questions, some of which she found impossible to answer. She pleaded with the public to keep their ears and eyes open and to ring the station if they saw two children fitting Tammy's and Ben's descriptions.

After the conference ended, Sara raced upstairs to the incident room to warn her team that the session had gone out live on the local BBC news, which she hadn't been expecting.

"I'm glad you've come in, boss, I was just about to send you a message," Jill said.

Sara could tell when Jill was excited about something, she always fidgeted in her chair. "What's up, Jill?"

"I took the liberty of digging into Abbott's background and I think I've found something important."

Sara motioned for her to continue.

"His grandparents died recently, leaving him a lot of money, over a hundred thousand. They also left him their cottage."

"What? Where is it?" Sara sank onto the desk behind her.

"It's over the border in Wales."

"Damn! How far over the border?"

"In Builth Wells."

"I've heard of it. Do you know how far it is?"

"Just over an hour away."

"Conceivable that he could be using the place to store the kids then, right?"

"Those are my thoughts, boss."

"Okay. I'll call a halt to the interview, and Carla and I will shoot over there. I could pass it on to someone else but I want to see for myself."

"I understand. Here's the address." Jill handed her a small piece of paper and smiled.

"Well done, Jill. Hopefully, this will be the last piece of the puzzle we need."

She ran back down the stairs and asked Carla to join her in the hallway.

"We might have an address. It's about an hour away. Let's fling him in a cell for now and shoot over there."

"Wow. Okay, is that likely? For him to keep the kids there?"

"We won't know until we get there. Let's get going. We need to check the ANPRs in the meantime, just in case. We'll get on the way, time being of the essence and all that."

*T*he cottage was at the end of a narrow country lane. The views across the nearby fields were magnificent. They were closer to Sara's beloved Brecon Beacons here.

"Look at that, stunning, isn't it?" she said.

"Are we really here to enjoy the views?"

"All right, sourpuss. I'm going to take a punt and see if there's a key under a pot, you know what old people are like."

Sara lifted a few pots decorated with dead plants sitting close to the front door and found nothing.

Carla winked at her and searched under the doormat and discovered the front door key. "You forgot to check the most obvious place."

"Old people never change, bless them." Heart pounding, Sara turned the key in the lock and eased open the door. It creaked a little. She flicked the switch by the front door. The room remained bleak and unforgiving. "No electricity."

"Great. Hang on." Carla shone the light from her torch around the room. "Yuck, this place hasn't been lived in for years. Look how dense those webs are. Oh fuck, I swear that spider just licked its damn lips. God, I'm going to be sick. The smell is atrocious."

"Stop complaining. We need to search this place, it shouldn't take long, it's tiny."

Carla held out her hand for Sara to shake. "What's the betting they're not here? Ten quid?"

"Not a gambling girl, you should know that." Sara removed her mobile from her pocket and switched the torch on. "That's better, I'll take upstairs this time."

"Thanks, do spiders go upstairs?"

"They do in our house. Get on with it."

The stairs groaned beneath her weight. Maybe she should have used the stairlift instead, although that looked fit enough only for being carted off to the knacker's yard, even then, it wouldn't have worked with no electricity. She reached the top and retched as the mustiness hit her nostrils. "Shit! No one could possibly survive in this place for long, not in this state." She shuddered and continued to search the tiny property. Being confronted by the one bedroom and small bathroom, Sara cringed at the state they were in and even managed to heave when she spotted how black the inside of the loo was.

She gave up and gingerly made her way back downstairs again. "Find anything?"

"Apart from several more spiders with wives and kiddies to boot, no, the place is empty."

"Bugger. All that way for nothing. If not here, then where's he keeping them?"

"*If* he has them at all. I have my doubts. You heard him pleading his innocence."

"Along with every other criminal we've ever questioned."

"I know. Maybe keeping him in a cell overnight will break him. Perhaps he'll be ready to give us a full confession in the morning."

"Is that a fairy in the garden?"

Carla craned her neck to peer out the little window overlooking the garden which resembled a jungle at the rear.

Sara slapped her. "I was kidding, numpty. I'm fed up with giving the analogy of pigs flying, thought I'd try something different instead."

"It didn't work, just like dragging us all the way out here didn't."

"We've got to check the garden yet. There could be an outbuilding or something, a well even, given our location."

"Do they have wells in this area?"

"What am I, a geography expert now?"

"There's no need to be snarky."

"Sorry, let's see what's out there. The light is beginning to fade. I don't relish searching by torchlight, it kills my eyes."

"That's because you're getting old."

Sara snubbed the comment and turned the huge key in the back door. The door had dropped and dragged on the lino floor below. Sara yanked it harder, and it gave way. "Bloody place needs demolishing. Can't see anyone injecting life into it."

"I suppose they'd need excessive funds to do that, which is why it's probably lying empty."

"True enough. I can't see anything out here. Wait, the garden is extended past the path. I'll check it out."

"Be careful, there could be snakes in that grass."

"Don't say that," Sara replied, hopping from one foot to the other.

Carla chuckled.

Sara tentatively walked the cobbled path until the curve. She paused and shone her torch. *Yes, there's a shed. Dare I look inside? I bet it's more infested with arachnids than the house.*

She was proved right. The door opened and disturbed another thick web, laden with dead flies and other creatures like wasps and daddy longlegs. She cringed again and peered into the darkness. Nothing in there but garden tools and a workbench. Definitely no children.

The trip had been a waste. Wearily, she retraced her steps back to the house and locked the door again. "Don't say it, let's get out of here."

"I told you so," Carla muttered when she thought Sara was out of earshot.

"I heard that. What's it like to always be right, partner?"

"I wouldn't know," Carla replied.

Disheartened, they replaced the key under the mat and returned to the station to inform the team. It had been a long day. Sara knew the villagers would be out there, doing their best to find the children. She made the call to send the team home early only to be reminded that the conference had aired and there were calls coming in. Thankfully, Will and Barry agreed to work until the phones died down.

"Thanks, guys. I need the break."

11

A much-deserved good night's sleep put the world to rights once more. Sara arrived back at the station an hour earlier than the rest of her team. She settled down to sort through the post and deal with any urgent paperwork just so it didn't lie heavily on her mind throughout the day. On the way in, she'd checked whether Abbott had had a comfortable night in his cell. The desk sergeant had told her he'd had a restless night, sobbed for most of it. Had that all been an act? She had her doubts.

"Morning, can I get you a coffee?" Carla poked her head into the room.

"Hey you, you look refreshed. Did you get a good eight hours in?"

"Around six. I take it you didn't. Looks like you've been here a while, am I correct?"

"You are. No lectures, and yes, a coffee would be wonderful."

"Coming right up."

She opened the last of her post as Carla placed her coffee on the desk.

"What's on the agenda today after yesterday's useless trip across the border?"

"I'll need to interview Abbott again this morning. In the meantime,

I'll get the team searching for any other possible locations where he might be holding the kids."

"Do you know if anything useful came from the press conference?" Carla sipped at her drink and leaned against the doorframe.

"Nothing much. One call about the red car being seen in the village. Obviously, we were aware of that. The next question is, how heavy should I be with Abbott? What if he clams up completely and we never find the kids?"

"Umm…it's not like you to be so defeatist."

"I know. I'm not usually. I can't help it running through my mind, though. I should check on Danny sometime during the day, too."

"Are you going to tell him about Abbott?"

"That's the ultimate dilemma, do I, or should I keep quiet in the hope that Abbott breaks down and confesses?"

"You'll know what's right once the time arrives."

"I hope so, I have huge doubts on this one."

"I'll leave you to it. Want me to make a start on Abbott's background checks?"

"If you don't mind. See if his parents are still alive and check where they live for starters."

Once Carla had left, Sara ran a hand around her aching neck and twisted it from side to side, hoping to relieve the tension that had built up already.

*T*he morning dragged by. Sara and Carla interviewed Abbott again, but he got so pissed off with being faced with the same questions that he clammed up completely and carried out his threat from the previous day and went down the 'no comment' route.

Sara threw him back in a cell, furious with her futile attempt and aware that time was running out for those kids. If he was their only lifeline…then a thought came to her: *if we release him, he could lead us right to them!*

She ran her wayward thought past the team, and they were in total agreement. However, DCI Price was having none of it.

"No. Do you want those kids' lives on your conscience, Inspector? What if you let him go, he panics and kills them, what then? How the heck do you think you're going to feel then?"

Suitably chastised, Sara had assured the chief she would hang on to the suspect and get the team working harder than they'd ever worked before to find the kids.

At one o'clock while the team were debating what to have for lunch, she received a call from the postman on Danny's route. "Oh God, no, it's happened again."

"Patrick? What are you talking about?"

"A dead body, no, two, you have to come, please."

Sara's eyes widened, and her heart pounded erratically. "Where? Where are you?"

"Shit! Out at Andy Brady's farm..."

"No. Jesus, okay. Stay there. I'm on my way. Don't touch anything, sit in your car."

"Oh fuck! The boss is going to kill me...again."

"He won't, I'll have a word. I'm heading out the door now."

"I'll see you soon."

He ended the call. "Shit! The postie has found two bodies out at Andy's farm, I'm presuming one of them is him. I want four of you out there with me and Carla, decide quickly. I need to ring the pathologist." She tore into her office to call Lorraine.

"Hi, and no, I haven't got any news for you. I might have this afternoon, though."

"I don't care. You need to get back out to Danny's place, more specifically his neighbour's farm. The other neighbour...oh shit, Andy Brady's property. The postie has just discovered two dead bodies, no idea who the victims are. I'm leaving now."

"Fuck. I'll gather the team. We'll be there soon."

Sara flew through the incident room. "All sorted?"

Carla nodded, and Barry, Craig, Marissa and Will were all standing in line ready to leave.

"What are we waiting for? Shit, please don't let this be Andy and where are the two PCs I left there, watching over him?"

Carla checked with the desk sergeant during the drive. He told them he'd pulled them out so they could help search for the kids. Now he was drowning in guilt. *I'll need to have a word when I return.*

*U*nder the speed they accomplished using their sirens, the group made it out to the farm within twenty minutes. Sara yanked on the handbrake and darted out of the car as soon as she drew up. Carla leapt out after her. They stopped more than ten feet from the bodies. One of them was indeed Andy. The other victim was a female.

"I wonder who she is," Carla said in a hushed voice.

"Haven't got a clue. They've both been shot."

Andy had a bullet wound in the side of his head, and half his brains were splattered over the driveway. The woman had blood seeping from a wound to her stomach.

"Whoa! Looks like a murder-suicide to me, boss," Will voiced his opinion after he'd stopped abruptly beside her.

"You think?" she turned to ask.

He nodded.

"Let's leave the speculation to the pathologist, shall we? Organise a cordon—no one gets any closer to the bodies, you hear me? Cross-contamination and all that. Oh fuck, I need to check on Danny. Stay here, Carla, make sure everyone follows the rules. I'll be back in a tick."

She drove next door and found the farm quiet, a strange vehicle sitting on the drive. Maybe Danny had hired one. She knocked on the door, and a dishevelled and bewildered-looking Danny answered it. He seemed surprised to see her.

"Hi, Danny, can I come in for a sec? I have some news for you."

"No. I mean, it's not convenient. Not unless it's concerning Tammy and Ben." He glanced over his shoulder.

His jitteriness sent alarm bells ringing.

"What's going on? Has something happened?" she asked.

Without warning, he reached out and grabbed her arm. The movement was that harsh she felt something rip under her skin as if he'd dislocated her shoulder. "Ouch! What are you doing?"

He gulped and dragged her into the kitchen. "They're out there."

"Who are? The children? Who, Danny?"

"They are. The ones who are after me."

"How do you know that? Has someone approached you? Rung you? Is that it?"

"Yes, yes, that's it." His eyes took on a crazed expression, similar to a wild animal caught in a snare, not knowing what to do to free itself.

Sara's gaze drifted to the kitchen table. There was a bundle of money sitting on it, and down on the floor, beside one of the legs, was a holdall. She looked back at the table. On it, a letter from Lloyds Bank. She made out the words in capital letters: REPOSSESSION ORDER. She glanced back at Danny. His eyes had formed into tiny slits.

"What's going on?" she asked, a note of suspicion in her voice.

"I have to get away."

"But your children are still missing. About that, we think we have a suspect at the station. We're interviewing him, we have been since last night. I didn't want to ring you to build your hopes up."

He let out a manic laugh that seared through her mind, clearing it.

"Call yourself a good detective? What a joke that is."

She shook her head as disbelief swept through her. "It was you all along, wasn't it?"

"Now that's an improvement. Answer me honestly. Would you have figured it out if you hadn't shown up when you did?"

"Yes, I would have, given time. You would've slipped up sooner or later. I'm guessing that's the money you stole from Frank, right?"

He applauded her, slowly. "Bravo, Inspector. Now all you have to do is work out where my kids are." He smirked, baring his teeth.

"How could you scare them like that? Knowing they'd just lost their mother. How heartless and callous of you."

"That's me. Gillian found out the hard way. She's been guilty of being too trusting over the years. What a fool she was."

"So, it was a bomb? You planted it in your own damn car, why?"

"I did. Genius, eh? To think up a cunning plan, to fox you lot with. It's taken me months, no, years, to come up with something of this enormity. The time was right." He turned to look at the letter on the table.

"The bank was going to repossess the farm, so you decided to kill off your neighbours after you murdered your wife." She gasped. "You killed Andy and the other person today, didn't you? Go on, admit it?"

"I did. His wife came back yesterday. I was hoping you would put the murders down to either the guy who was threatening me or a murder-suicide. He was too friendly with Gillian, they both were."

"Both? Are you talking about Frank?"

"Yes. They always treated her well and ignored me as if I wasn't good enough to be a member of the farming community."

"Maybe they were right, if this is the end result. Why kill them?"

"Why not? Gillian was leaving me, taking the kids with her. I had to bring my plans forward and alter them once I realised she was about to do a runner."

Sara pointed at him. "Her brakes, you cut her brakes in the hope she'd have an accident and get killed. When that didn't work, you rigged up the bomb. I'm right, aren't I?"

He smirked and nodded. There was amusement shining in his eyes. Sara resisted the urge to shudder under his watchful gaze. *How could I have been so wrong about him? How?*

"So, where are the children? Have you killed them?"

"No. I could never kill them, they have my genes running through them. They're the only thing I've done right over the years, according to my deceased wife. She flung that at me regularly. She wasn't innocent in all of this. She nagged me to get involved in the community. I tried my hardest, but the bastards kept rejecting me. They saw me as an outsider. Well, I showed them all what I was capable of in the end. They should've given me a chance. They didn't, refused to do it, and there was only one thing left for me to do…punish them. All of them. I hid the kids to make the threats seem more realistic."

"I get that, no matter how warped I think you were putting them through it. And your neighbours? Why them? You didn't have to do that."

He leaned into her. "I've just told you why, they detested me. So I taught them both a lesson. I don't have time for this, I have plans."

"Where are you holding the children?" Her gaze drifted to the latched door off to the side.

He laughed again. "I saw you notice it the other day. What did you think it was? A pantry?"

"Yes, don't tell me it's a cellar?"

"All right, I won't, but it is." As quick as a flash, he pulled a knife out and pointed it at her throat. "My plan keeps altering every time a new situation arises."

"My team are only next door. It's only a matter of time before they come looking for me."

He dug into her pocket and removed her phone. He let it drop on the tiled floor and then ground his heel into it. The screen smashed, exposing the onboard computer.

Shit! Bang goes my chance of getting out of here alive.

Something came down heavily on her head. She dropped to her knees, and then darkness overwhelmed her.

*S*ara regained consciousness, unsure where she was at first until realisation dawned. Lying on the kitchen floor amongst the crumbs and tea stains, she tried to move her arms but failed. They were tied behind her back. *Bugger! What now?*

The door to the cellar was open. Danny's voice echoed up the stair-well, along with the kids' screams. She had to help them, there was no telling what this maniac would be likely to do next. Although he'd already stated he wouldn't hurt them, by the sounds of it, it was another one of his bare-faced lies. Panic-stricken, she surveyed the room. There was nothing down at this level to help her, nothing she could rub up against to free her hands.

She had a small penknife attached to her car keys, but there was no point thinking about that now, they were sitting in her ignition.

How the hell am I supposed to save the children if I can't even save myself?

Footsteps, two or maybe three sets coming up the stairs. She squeezed her eyes shut, pretending to be unconscious.

The two children screamed again once they came into the kitchen.

"You think you can fool me? I can tell you're awake," Danny shouted.

"Let us go, all of us. I'll make sure I have a word in your favour at the hearing."

"Why would I want to do that? You think I'm scared of killing an officer of the law? Why should that bother me after what I've done to the others?"

"Don't do it. Just let the kids and me go…"

"Shut the fuck up. Yes, Ben, Daddy swore. It's not the first time you've heard me swear and it won't be the last. She's a pest, we need to get rid of her. I'm going to put you all in the car while I have a think about this."

Sara kept her mouth shut. As long as he didn't kill her here, there was hope of someone being able to track them down. How, she didn't know, not now her phone had been destroyed. Could she leave a trail, a clue of sorts for someone to find? Her team were sure to come looking for her if she didn't return to Andy's farm soon. At least she hoped they would.

He told the kids to sit at the table and not to move. Then he hoisted Sara off the floor and onto his shoulder. He carried her out to the car and threw her onto the back seat. She cried out, the pain ripping through her already injured shoulder.

"Oops, did I hurt you?" He backed out of the car and returned to the house.

Sara struggled to sit up. She twisted her wrists in an attempt to loosen what she thought was garden twine wrapped several times around her wrists for added strength. It proved to be a dismal attempt. He reappeared, carrying Tammy, who was crying, and holding Ben's hand. The little lad was beside himself, walking as if he had robotic features. Her heart went out to the kids. They were too young to deal with this crap. What sort of father would knowingly put his kids through such distress? *The same type who wouldn't think twice about killing their mother. Shame on him.*

Danny placed the kids in the car with a stark warning not to move. He ran back inside the house, presumably to grab the bag and money.

"Are you all right, children?" She smiled at them, trying to break through their barrier of fear.

Ben glanced up at her. He wriggled in his seat, grappling behind him for something. Then, to Sara's utter surprise and delight, he held up a knife. The only trouble was it was a normal cutlery knife, not a sharp kitchen knife. It didn't matter, it was worth a try.

"Good lad, can you cut the twine, Ben?" Sara twisted in her seat to give him access to her wrists. The knife slipped against her hand now and again. She refused to gasp, fearing the boy wouldn't want to continue if he thought he was hurting her.

"Here, let me have a go," Tammy said.

"I know. Can you both do it together?" Sara asked, thinking the extra force might help.

"I think we can," Ben replied eagerly.

Sara continued to twist her wrists, not caring if the knife or the coarse twine did any damage to her skin—it would be negligible if it did. A few strands frayed under the children's joint effort. "It's working, hurry, quickly before he comes back."

Sara's neck was hurting as she strained to peer over her shoulder at the farmhouse. *What's taking him so long? Not that I'm complaining. Come on kids, do your stuff.*

The kids huffed and puffed, their exertions proving to be too much for them.

"My hand hurts," Ben cried.

"Okay, I'll finish. You rest," Tammy replied.

"You're doing great. Keep going. You can do it, Tammy," Sara urged.

"My hands hurt as well," Tammy said after a few seconds.

"I can help again," Ben chimed in.

A few more twists, and the rope snapped. Sara shot out of the car and grabbed the children. Together they bolted towards one of the barns. Hopefully he wouldn't see in which direction they were heading out of one of the windows. It was a long shot, she knew. She plumped for the barn where the machinery was stored, knowing that it was full of nooks and crannies where she could hide the children while she dealt with their father.

The children hid beneath a small tractor and some form of plough attachment, in separate locations, in the hope that it would prolong the search for them and give Sara extra time to either attack Danny or come up with a plan to get them all out of there alive.

She armed herself with a couple of heavy wrenches. It was all she had time to source before the crunching gravel heralded his approaching feet.

"You're dancing with danger, Inspector. Show yourself and I'll consider letting you go. I know you're in here. Underestimating me will be your undoing, I'm warning you. Tammy, Ben, come to Daddy and I won't punish you. Instead, I'll give you a month's supply of sweeties over the weekend." His voice had developed a singsong element to it to try to coax the kids out of their hidey-holes.

It was far too late for that; he was an idiot if he anticipated bribing them with sweets would make them show themselves after what he'd done to their mother.

Sara found a bolt and tossed it to the rear of the barn, in the opposite direction to where she and the children were hiding. He fell for it and tore a path through the machinery, casting some of the tools and equipment aside in his determination to get to them. Sara had a clear view of him, his face now contorted with rage, his cheeks enflamed.

"Come out here, kids. You have until I count to five…if you're not out by then…you'll be sorry."

Sara stared at the kids and held a finger up to her lips and shook her head. Petrified, they stared back at her and both nodded.

A gun fired. The sound ricocheted around the barn. Ben let out a shriek. Sara closed her eyes for a second, willing Danny not to have noticed his son's moment of betrayal. He had. Danny stormed over to where his son was hiding and yanked him from his secure place.

He held his son in front of him, his arm around his throat. Ben tried to prise his father's arm away, allowing him to breathe.

"You're hurting me," the boy cried out, his voice constricted by his father's firm hold.

"Shut up. Come out, Inspector, or I'll shoot him. Kill him so he can be with his mother."

The next second, Tammy broke free from her hiding place. Sara's heart seemed to hit her stomach. *Fuck! This wasn't supposed to happen. If I show myself, he'll kill me.*

He held up his gun with his free hand and shot off a couple of rounds. "I still have a couple left, they have Tammy's and Ben's names on them." *I hope the team hear the shots, or is that wishful thinking?*

"No, Daddy, please, let us go. We haven't done anything wrong," Tammy pleaded. She struggled with her father, trying to loosen his grip on her brother. She kicked out at Danny's shin which earnt her a slap.

Tammy fell to the floor.

Her father towered over her and, glowering, he shouted, "Just like your mother. Always think you're right. Stay there. Move and I'll shoot you."

Sara debated her next move but only for an instant. He was hurting the kids which didn't sit well with her. She revealed herself, coming out with her hands raised. "Okay, we'll do as you say, just don't hurt the kids."

"Thought you could outwit me, did you? You were wrong. I told you, I'm a planner, I rarely get things wrong. Get over here."

Tentatively, Sara edged between the machinery towards him. Something caught her eye, but her gaze remained focused on Danny. She lowered her hands the closer she got to him. "Let me have Ben."

He shoved his son at her. "You're welcome to hi—" He failed to complete his sentence, hard to do with fifty thousand volts coursing through your body.

"Daddy," Tammy shouted.

Sara pounced on the child, fearing Tammy might touch her father and receive a shock herself. "Don't touch him. He'll be fine. Stunned, that's all. Are you all right, sweetie?"

Ben hugged her legs while Tammy rose to her feet and latched on to her brother.

"You saved us," Ben shouted over and over.

Sara kept their attention focused on her until their father's body lay still on the floor as Carla, Taser in hand, and Will rushed into the barn.

"Boy, am I glad to see you two," Sara told them, a relieved smile pulling her lips apart.

"Are you all right? All of you?" Carla touched Sara's arm and ruffled Ben's hair.

Sara sighed. "We'll be fine, won't we, kids?"

Tammy leaned back and glanced up at her. "Will we? Who will look after us now?"

"Don't worry, we'll sort that out later, love. You're safe, that's all that matters for now."

Sara and Carla led the kids out of the barn while Will saw to their father. He cuffed him and removed the Taser wires from his back. Danny was groggy but still alive.

Good, I'd hate for him to have died. He needs to be punished for what he's put his kids through and the murders he's committed over the past few days.

"How did you know I was in trouble?" Sara took a sip of water from the bottle Carla had handed to her.

"The shots. Once we heard them, Will insisted you were in trouble and needed our help."

"Good old Will. I'll be forever in your debt. This was a close one. He's unstable, he has to be after what he put his own kids through."

"Shh…don't let him hear you say that, otherwise he'll take the insanity route and we'll never get justice for his victims."

EPILOGUE

*W*hen Sara returned to the murder scene at Andy's farm, Lorraine rushed up to her. Concerned, she asked, "Are you all right? The guys just told me what happened to you. Let me look at you. Oh my, your wrists are cut to ribbons, I'll get the first-aid kit out of the van."

Sara chuckled. "Stop fussing like a mother hen. I'm fine, they're superficial wounds."

"How did you get them?"

She ran through the events that led up to her wounds. Lorraine's mouth hung open all the time she spoke.

"What brave kids. Anyway, remember when we spoke this morning and I told you I'd get back to you this afternoon? Well, I have news that will probably come as no surprise to you after what's developed this afternoon."

"I'm all ears. Don't tell me you have DNA evidence against Danny?"

"And some," Lorraine replied. "First of all, we found a fingerprint of Danny's on Frank's gun. Secondly, with regard to the explosion—"

"It was definitely a bomb, he admitted as much to me. Not only that, if your guys inspect the barn over there, I noticed a bunch of ball bearings scattered across the floor. I'm betting there were some in the crude bomb he made, am I right?"

"Wow, yes, you're correct. What a bastard. Rigging the bomb up would have taken him hours, if not days to do."

"He had all the time in the world. Sneaky little shit. It winds me up how many people kill their bloody spouses instead of just setting them free. They hadn't been happy for a while, according to her best friend, and Gillian was getting ready to leave him and travel up to Cumbria to be with her sister. Which reminds me, I need to ring her, see if she'll come and collect the kids."

"I repeat, what a bastard. You do that. That's all the news I have anyway."

"It's great that we have some evidence to confront him with during the interview."

*B*ack at the station, Sara interviewed Danny. He glared at her the whole time. Started off denying all the charges laid against him, of four counts of murder and the abduction of Tammy and Ben, that was until Sara presented him with the incriminating evidence.

He buckled and, backed into a corner, he admitted everything.

"Why kill Gillian?"

"Because I found a suitcase in the loft last week. I opened it to find all her newest clothes inside, so I knew it wasn't just being stored up there out of the way. I knew she was going to leave me."

"Why not just let her go?"

"Why should she be allowed to leave when we were both guilty of getting the farm in a mess?"

"The bank was about to take it off you, weren't they?"

"Yes, I couldn't allow that. I'd worked hard to try and make that place pay. It's not my fault the price of lamb has dropped to an all-time low, is it?"

"But to kill your wife and then to go on to kill Andy, his wife and Frank, why?"

"I told you, they refused to accept me."

"And the notes? Before you try to deny it, SOCO found a notebook in your lounge with identical paper. There were indents on the pad so they used the scientific method of scribbling over it with a pencil and, lo and behold, the imprint of the last note you were supposedly sent came through. It was all a ruse, wasn't it?"

He shrugged and grinned. "It kept you all guessing, didn't it?"

"And the ewe, was that real or was that all a fabrication to gain my sympathy?"

"No, it was real. I needed to vent my anger one day…"

"So you killed two of your flock, even though money was tight?"

"It made me feel better."

"I'm done here, we have your confession. Wait, one last thing. How did you abduct the children and allow Victor to find you? Where did you put the kids?"

He smirked and wiggled his eyebrows. "That was a cunning part of the plan. I pulled a blinder with that one, didn't I?"

"How?" Sara insisted.

"I put the kids on the other side of the hedge and warned them what I would do to them if they either came out or made a noise. They're used to me issuing threats and punishing them if they do anything wrong. I confused them further by wearing a mask in the cellar. They didn't know it was me."

"Jesus, you're one sick…and the cut to your head?"

"I did that, too. I convinced you and your partner here. Good, ain't I?"

Sara bit back the anger threatening to erupt. "Not good enough, obviously. Otherwise you wouldn't have got caught. You're going to go away for a long time, Danny. I hope you deem all your planning worthwhile now, because I can tell you this, it definitely contributed to your downfall. Interview ended."

Sara walked out of the room with her head held high and left Carla to complete the interview and to throw Danny back in his temporary cell.

Jeff poked his head around the corner at the end of the hallway. "I have someone to see you, ma'am."

"I'm coming." She entered the reception area and held her hand out to the woman sitting in the seat next to the door. "Hello, Philomena, thank you for coming. I'm Sara Ramsey."

"Pleased to meet you. Are the children here?"

"No, they stayed with foster parents last night. They're very shaken up as you can imagine."

"Has the bastard said why he killed my sister?"

"It's been building for months, apparently. The final straw came when he found a packed suitcase in the loft."

"Damn, I told her to put it up there out of the way. This is all my fault." She covered her face and cried.

Sara rubbed her arm. "You mustn't think like that. All you did was supply a way out. I'm glad you've offered to take the kids on, to give them some stability."

Philomena dropped her hands, wiped her eyes on a tissue and said, "I would never let them down. I'll give them as good a life as their mother would have. I'll make sure they remember her and how much she loved them."

She gasped. Sara looked over her shoulder to find Carla strolling past with Danny. His demented laughter drifted down the corridor long after Carla forced him to continue walking.

"What a callous man. I've always hated him," Philomena said.

"He's a hell of a disturbed guy, that's for sure. I'm glad the kids will be with someone who cares about them."

"Thank you for putting your life on the line to save them."

"It was nothing. All in a day's work and part of the job."

THE END

*W*ell that was another gripping investigation for Sara and her team to sink their teeth into. I hope you enjoyed it? If you did, then perhaps you'll consider leaving a review as they brighten an author's darkest days when imposter syndrome strikes.

Grab your copy of the next book in the series, **Sign of Evil** now.

Perhaps you'd also consider reading another of my most popular series? Grab the first book in the Justice series here, CRUEL JUSTICE

DI Sara Ramsey will return in Sign of Evil, a brand new case, early in 2021.

KEEP IN TOUCH WITH THE AUTHOR

Pick up a FREE novella by signing up to my newsletter today.
https://BookHip.com/WBRTGW

BookBub
www.bookbub.com/authors/m-a-comley

Blog
http://melcomley.blogspot.com

Join my special Facebook group to take part in monthly giveaways.

Readers' Group